Khalil lunged from the chair, knocking Bolan's gun aside

The terrorist's momentum drove him into the Executioner, and as he attempted to regain his balance, he felt Khalil's fingers free the handgun tucked behind his belt.

The man's face wore an expression of triumph as he began to line up a shot. As Bolan fell, he clamped the big .44 Magnum in both fists, tracking the muzzle on his adversary's torso and pulling the trigger.

The large-caliber slugs chewed into the terrorist's chest, driving him backward into the window that overlooked the beach. The glass shattered, and the man fell onto the balcony.

Bolan gained his feet, aware of a stinging pain across his upper arm where Khalil's bullet had left a ragged tear. He moved to the window, looking down at the corpse.

The Executioner had come out on top in this confrontation, but Khalil's death had also removed any chance of finding out the location of the Disciples of Khalfi's next hit.

MACK BOLAN ®

The Executioner

#152 Combat Stretch
#153 Firebase Florida
#154 Night Hit
#155 Hawaiian Heat
#156 Phantom Force
#157 Cayman Strike
#158 Firing Line
#159 Steel and Flame
#160 Storm Warning
#161 Eye of the Storm
#162 Colors of Hell
#163 Warrior's Edge
#164 Death Trail
#165 Fire Sweep
#166 Assassin's Creed
#167 Double Action
#168 Blood Price
#169 White Heat
#170 Baja Blitz
#171 Deadly Force
#172 Fast Strike
#173 Capitol Hit
#174 Battle Plan
#175 Battle Ground
#176 Ransom Run
#177 Evil Code
#178 Black Hand
#179 War Hammer
#180 Force Down
#181 Shifting Target
#182 Lethal Agent
#183 Clean Sweep
#184 Death Warrant
#185 Sudden Fury
#186 Fire Burst
#187 Cleansing Flame

#188 War Paint
#189 Wellfire
#190 Killing Range
#191 Extreme Force
#192 Maximum Impact
#193 Hostile Action
#194 Deadly Contest
#195 Select Fire
#196 Triburst
#197 Armed Force
#198 Shoot Down
#199 Rogue Agent
#200 Crisis Point
#201 Prime Target
#202 Combat Zone
#203 Hard Contact

DON PENDLETON'S
THE EXECUTIONER®
HARD CONTACT

A GOLD EAGLE BOOK FROM

WORLDWIDE®

TORONTO • NEW YORK • LONDON
AMSTERDAM • PARIS • SYDNEY • HAMBURG
STOCKHOLM • ATHENS • TOKYO • MILAN
MADRID • WARSAW • BUDAPEST • AUCKLAND

First edition November 1995
ISBN 0-373-64203-2

Special thanks and acknowledgment to
Michael Linaker for his contribution to this work.

HARD CONTACT

My honor is dearer to me than my life.
—Miguel de Cervantes
1547–1616

There is no honor in slaughter, no glory in the
indiscriminate murder of innocent people.
—Mack Bolan

THE
MACK BOLAN®
LEGEND

Nothing less than a war could have fashioned the destiny of the man called Mack Bolan. Bolan earned the Executioner title in the jungle hell of Vietnam.

But this soldier also wore another name—Sergeant Mercy. He was so tagged because of the compassion he showed to wounded comrades-in-arms and Vietnamese civilians.

Mack Bolan's second tour of duty ended prematurely when he was given emergency leave to return home and bury his family, victims of the Mob. Then he declared a one-man war against the Mafia.

He confronted the Families head-on from coast to coast, and soon a hope of victory began to appear. But Bolan had broken society's every rule. That same society started gunning for this elusive warrior—to no avail.

So Bolan was offered amnesty to work within the system against terrorism. This time, as an employee of Uncle Sam, Bolan became Colonel John Phoenix. With a command center at Stony Man Farm in Virginia, he and his new allies—Able Team and Phoenix Force—waged relentless war on a new adversary: the KGB.

But when his one true love, April Rose, died at the hands of the Soviet terror machine, Bolan severed all ties with Establishment authority.

Now, after a lengthy lone-wolf struggle and much soul-searching, the Executioner has agreed to enter an "arm's-length" alliance with his government once more, reserving the right to pursue personal missions in his Everlasting War.

PROLOGUE

It was a quarter to twelve when David McCarter spotted the man named Ariq walking swiftly along the rain-swept Marseilles waterfront. The tall British member of Stony Man's Phoenix Force felt relief wash over him. He'd been waiting for Ariq for more than three hours. He was wet, cold and in a foul mood. His condition wasn't improved by the fact that he had run out of cigarettes. Easing back into the shadows, McCarter removed the compact transceiver concealed inside his leather jacket and keyed the transmit button.

"Watcher Two to Watcher One. Over."

The clipped tones of Yakov Katzenelenbogen responded.

"Watcher One receiving. Over."

"Our wandering bird has come home," McCarter said. "Now can we get this bloody show on the road before I die of exposure? Over."

"All right, Two. Go in now. All the exits are covered. One out."

McCarter put away the handset, replacing it with his Browning Hi-Power 9 mm pistol. He eased off the safety as he slipped from the shadows and crossed the narrow alley, going through the brick archway in

Ariq's footsteps. The dimly lit passage led to a flight of stone steps that ran up the side of the grimy building. McCarter took the steps two at a time, pausing on the landing. There was a single door in front of him, partially open. The Phoenix Force commando toed the door open, peering into the musty-smelling hallway, which was lit by a single bulb dangling from a frayed cord. Old paint on the walls and ceiling was cracked and peeling, stained from dampness.

"Home sweet home," McCarter muttered as he slipped in through the door, wrinkling his nose at the sour smell pervading the air.

He made for the stairs leading to the upper floor, where he knew Ariq had gone. McCarter climbed them quickly, keeping to the inside wall. He had checked the stairs earlier and was aware of telltale creaks that might give him away to anyone listening. He reached the head of the stairs and crossed to the door of the apartment Ariq was using. He pressed his back to the wall to the left of the door and took out the transceiver. All he did this time was to key the transmit button three times, a prearranged signal to alert the others that he was in position.

Taking a deep breath, McCarter turned to face the door. He raised his right foot and drove it forward, striking just below the handle. The door burst open, slamming back against the inside wall. The Briton entered, ducking low and breaking to the right, shoulders against the inside wall, the Browning held in both hands and tracking ahead of him as he scanned the room: cheap furnishings and drab decor; a threadbare carpet on the floor; a door off to his right that led into a kitchen; off to his left, doors to the bedroom and bathroom.

That was it—except for the naked man bound to a wooden chair in the center of the room, the man Phoenix Force had been looking for.

The captive was an undercover Mossad operative who had been liaising with Stony Man for the past couple of months, helping them track an Islamic terrorist splinter group. He had vanished from sight more than three days earlier, and it had taken Phoenix Force that long to pick up the trail, latching on to Ariq, a Marseilles-based member of the terrorist group responsible for intelligence and weapons supply for the group's European operations. They had located his safehouse and had waited for him to come back so they could isolate him in his apartment.

What they hadn't expected was to find their missing man there.

The bound man, heavily gagged, stared across the room at McCarter, recognition flickering in his pain-dulled eyes.

McCarter had seen the bloody marks of torture on the man's naked body, the dark stains crusting the carpet at his feet.

In that instant the bound man's eyes rolled to one side, signaling desperately.

McCarter turned, catching a glimpse of sudden, blurred movement coming into his field of vision.

Ariq lunged at him, lamplight bouncing off the blade of the long knife cutting the air close to McCarter's throat. Only the effort of arching back drew the Briton's flesh away from the razor edge.

McCarter struck the wall, using the impact to push himself forward again, slamming bodily against Ariq. His left hand swept up, fingers clamping around Ariq's knife wrist. Then the Phoenix Force commando slammed the Browning against Ariq's skull, the man grunting as the hard steel drove fingers of pain through his head. He made an attempt to wrench his wrist free, but McCarter hung on grimly. He brought his right arm around in a vicious forearm smash that thudded against the side of the terrorist's face, spinning the man off balance.

As Ariq stumbled, McCarter kicked him hard in the ribs, knocking him across the room. Ariq fell hard, but kept a grip on the knife. He scrambled to his knees, his bloody face showing a wild grin as he thrust his knife forward again.

As fast as he was, the Briton was faster. The lanky Phoenix commando had closed in quickly, and he met Ariq as the terrorist pulled himself upright. McCarter's left fist lashed out and took the man under the jaw with enough force to break bone. Ariq let out a weak groan as he was driven to the floor. This time the knife bounced from his nerveless fingers. McCarter kicked it across the room as he bent and hauled his adversary off the floor by the collar of his coat as the terrorist clawed for another weapon. He swung Ariq headfirst against the wall, where the man jerked briefly, his body abruptly losing all its resistance as his neck snapped.

Turning to the bound man McCarter removed the gag.

"Have you out of here in a few minutes, chum."

The Mossad agent gulped in deep breaths.

"Don't waste time talking," McCarter said.

"In his inside pocket," the Israeli said. "Envelope with a sheet of paper."

McCarter located the envelope. He took out the folded paper, which was covered with Arabic script.

"What is it?" he asked.

"I'll translate," the Mossad agent said as McCarter untied him. He took the paper in his bruised and bloody hands and began to read in English.

"Bloody hell!" McCarter finally said.

He took out his transceiver and thumbed the transmit button.

"Get up here, guys. The situation is clear, but we need to get a message home fast. And I mean fast!"

BROGNOLA SLID the typed sheet across the table and watched Bolan scan it.

"That's a translation," the big Fed explained. "The original came via Phoenix Force. McCarter got his hands on it after taking out a guy named Ariq. He was the local contact man for a terrorist group that followed—in fact, still follows—one of the ayatollahs, a guy called Khalfi. Remember him?"

Bolan nodded. He took his eyes off the paper.

"Yeah, I remember him. Khalfi was a hard-liner. He had a heavy downer on anything and everything that wasn't in line with Islam. Leaned toward the extreme, even with his own followers."

"Something of a fire-eater," Brognola agreed. "One hundred percent fundamentalist. No wavering. He had a big following. There was even a protection squad made up from his most fervent brethren, who called themselves the Disciples of Khalfi."

"And they're still active," Bolan said, tapping the sheet of paper, "even though Khalfi is long dead."

"You got it, Striker."

"And this was the group Phoenix Force was checking out?"

"Yeah. Israeli Intelligence picked up on them some months back. They tracked them into Europe where they were setting up a network. They had links with Libyan cells, even the IRA. Seems they were in the market for weapons and explosives. Intel from Mossad suggested the Disciples of Khalfi had specific aims, including anything and everything U.S. This was more or less confirmed by a spate of killings of Americans working in Europe. We kept the lid on everything while it was checked out. And it did, unfortunately. The Disciples of Khalfi claimed responsibility, saying this was only the beginning. America would pay in blood for what had been done to Ayatollah Khalfi. Everything they did was in his name, for his memory and for God."

"They didn't specify their next target?" Bolan asked.

Brognola shook his head, toying with his coffee mug.

"Not until now. According to this document there's a cell in the U.S. set to carry out more executions, against a media news team.

"Why?" Bolan asked.

"Let me explain the background to all this, Mack," Brognola said. He got up to stretch his legs and crossed to where a simmering coffeepot sat on a heated plate. After pouring himself a mug, the big Fed returned to his seat.

"Two months before Khalfi died, the news team made a TV documentary about him. It was some coup, the first time any Western media people had even gotten close. They were on the edge with every piece they filmed, following Khalfi around on one of his tours. For some reason known only to himself, Khalfi allowed them a couple of short interviews. Good news for the team, but it didn't sit too well with Khalfi's critics back home. By the time he got back he was already being accused of betraying Islam by talking to representatives of the Western media.

"When the film was eventually shown, it made an impact from here to the Gulf. Khalfi came out as an extremist who appeared to be pushing too hard and going against the wishes of the masses. Exiles from Iran had also been interviewed, and Khalfi's reputation was put into doubt. It was balanced reportage but not what Khalfi's camp wanted to see and hear. The moderates were angry because it damaged the good works they had been doing.

"Khalfi might have handled that in the long run. He was used to being hauled over the coals for his ultraextremist views and demands. But the ones who wanted him out—and there were a few—latched on to this episode and started a heavy campaign. The whole thing got out of hand then and ended up as one hell of an internecine struggle, with one faction against another. Rallies turned into open battles between the opposing sides. The upshot was quite a few people dead, and Khalfi himself blown up by a bomb planted in his house."

"Set by his opponents?"

"We'll never really know," Brognola admitted. "Intelligence picked up a story going around that we planted the bomb ourselves. According to the leak, it was a conspiracy between U.S. undercover agents and terrorists opposed to Islam."

"Whichever way it reads, we come out the bad guys."

"It's the world we live in," Brognola said, sighing. "After Khalfi died he was replaced by a young ayatollah named Numar. We didn't have much on him, but it appears he was a follower of Khalfi from day one, and he rallied support from the old ayatollah's faithful. It seems this Numar is a smart boy. He has an answer for everything and keeps his ear to the ground. Before we know it, he's up and running the show. He touts Khalfi as the ultimate martyr and pins the blame on the U.S. and the news team in particular. He needed something he could focus attention on, so he chose the media and really went to work on them. But we weren't sure how he was going to play it until Phoenix Force came up with the document they found in Marseilles."

"You figure this Numar is pulling the strings and the Disciples are dancing for him?"

"I think he lit the fuse and set them free," Brognola replied. "What this means, Mack, is a bunch of terrorists on American soil, a damned hit team out to assassinate American citizens in their own country. We let that happen, and we'll have every organization with a grievance doing the same."

Bolan stood, pushing his chair aside.

"Not as long as I have anything to say about it," he said. "Hal, how fresh is this information from Phoenix Force?"

"Straight off the wire," the big Fed stated.

"Who else knows about it?"

"Only those who need to. I spoke with the President just before you arrived. We agreed this has to be kept in-house. We take it on board solo so we can keep it under control. If word gets out there's a hit team running free in the country, every cop between here and Nome, Alaska, will be in there trying to nail them. Mack, I want these loose cannons out of action fast."

"Do we have locations on the news team?"

"Aaron is working on that right now. It looks like they've split up since the Khalfi film. The only one we have any trace on is Ras Fallil. He's a Muslim himself and has been in the country for over ten years. He's a U.S. citizen now and lives in New York."

"Then I'll start with him," Bolan said, pushing to his feet.

"Hal, get me all the information you can. I'm heading for New York."

BY THE TIME Mack Bolan reached New York, checking in by telephone, Brognola had information for him—but not the kind he wanted to hear.

Ras Fallil had been located, dead. His bullet-riddled body had been found in his car, parked near the East River.

Brognola had pulled rank over the local authorities, keeping news of Fallil's death quiet for as long as he could. The New York police were advised it was a hands-off situation, which they didn't like but were forced to accept in the short term.

It gave Bolan breathing space, time to check out Ras Fallil's apartment in Greeenwich Village before the local cops moved in.

1

Death and Mack Bolan were old adversaries. They had sparred many times before, and would do so again in the future. This time the battleground was New York City. Death threw out its challenge in the familiar form of a suppressed 9 mm bullet that cleaved the air between it and the intended target.

Warned of its coming by the soft click of sound from a safety being released, Bolan turned aside in the fraction of a second before the suppressed gun fired. The bullet tore a ragged splinter of wood from the door frame, spitting fragments at the Executioner's right cheek.

Then he was down on one knee, his upper body half turned toward the source of the sound. His right arm came up, fingers gripping the butt of the Beretta 93-R, set for 3-round bursts, and sought his target. The warrior's keen eyes picked out the shadowed form across the shadowed room, his finger stroking the trigger as the 93-R tracked in. The pistol chugged its triple burst and the target was held in midstride, the gunner gasping in shock. Then he performed a silent, grisly pirouette before crashing heavily to the carpeted floor.

Bolan was already on the move, skirting the edge of the wall as he searched for the man's partner. The Beretta moved before him, the muzzle restless as it crisscrossed the room, never still as it searched for its next target.

The man gave himself away, maybe because he was nervous at seeing his partner go down so quickly, perhaps greedy to claim a hit for his own gratification. But still careless. And the carelessness came with a high price tag.

The merest whisper of clothing disturbed by movement reached the Executioner's ears. He remained where he was, only his eyes moving, registering the dark bulk on the far side of the room. The man stepped to one side and placed himself in front of the drawn window blind. The halo of subdued light around his form gave Bolan a perfect target.

Bolan carefully brought the 93-R to bear. Then he aimed and fired in a single, fluid gesture. The triple burst caught the guy in the upper chest, near the shoulder. He yelled and fell back, slumping against the wall, the stubby subgun spilling from his fingers as he clasped both hands to his wound.

Crossing the room Bolan crouched by the first man he had taken out. A swift check verified that the guy was dead. Blood was pooling around the body, soaking into the pile of the carpet. He picked up the gunner's weapon and dropped out the magazine, kicking it across the room.

Proceeding to the second gunner, he removed the discarded subgun. The guy was still alive, bleeding profusely from the pulpy wound in his upper chest. He stared at Bolan from watery eyes, puffing in ragged gasps from a slack mouth. His face gleamed with sweat.

Keeping the Beretta trained on the guy's face Bolan frisked him. He found an autopistol inside the man's creased jacket and a switchblade knife in his pocket.

"I will not tell you a thing," the man said suddenly. "You can do what you will. God is my witness. I would die rather than allow the words to pass my lips."

Bolan glanced at the man. Black hair flopped limply across his face as he glowered at the Executioner. His outburst seemed to have bolstered his confidence. Hate burned in his dark eyes. Bolan had seen that intense stare before, the look of the dedicated. Some would say fanatic. However he was judged, the wounded man would hate with a vengeance. Its intensity would overcome his pain and make him dangerous—in the extreme, Bolan realized, as the lean figure erupted from the base of the wall.

Burning with some inner force, the wounded man threw himself at Bolan, catching the Executioner momentarily off balance. A hard shoulder slammed into Bolan's chest, driving him backward.

Before he could recover, the raging figure turned away from him—not toward him—and took three long strides before launching himself in a headlong dive through the covered window. Glass shattered, the thin blind protecting the man's flesh as he crashed down on the fire escape outside.

By the time Bolan reached the window, dragging aside the shredded blind, the gunman had vanished down the iron ladder, melting into the darkness of the rainy night.

Turning back into the room Bolan located a lamp and switched it on. The spread of illumination revealed the room to have been wrecked. Drawers had been dragged open and the contents strewn across the floor. Books and tapes had been tossed aside as someone searched for some hidden object. Furniture lay in broken pieces, some upended.

The warrior crossed to the dead man, crouched beside the body and went through the man's pockets. They held the usual contents: money, credit cards and a driver's license that most probably held phony information. Bolan took it for checking.

From the inside pocket of the dead man's coat, Bolan pulled out a folded slip of paper on which were written two items: a telephone number and a name.

Something else for the Stony Man computers to check on.

Bolan had come to New York seeking the man who had owned this apartment, someone linked to his mission. By the time he had arrived in the city, the man was dead, murdered. With the man dead, Bolan had taken the logical step of checking out his apartment.

Others had been struck by the same thought, violent people who were willing to kill without hesitation because Bolan had walked in on them searching a dead man's apartment.

New York had a reputation as a vibrant, explosive city. Within its narrow confines were contained millions of restless individuals. The city lived on a thin edge, often spilling over into violence. Bolan had walked off the streets and had stepped directly into the line of fire. Unlike most ordinary people, he was capable of responding to such threats, and of taking the situation that one step further. He had clashed with the enemy. They would know of his presence now and would act accordingly. Bolan wanted that, needed them to be aware that he was tracking them. Any complacency they might have had before was no longer valid. They would now be on the defensive, looking over their shoulders every now and then.

And sooner or later Mack Bolan would be there.

The numbers were already falling. Time was slipping away, and the Executioner was on target.

THE TELEPHONE was answered on the third ring.

"Yes?"

"It is me. Raffi. We have been compromised. We were at Fallil's apartment looking for information. Someone came. I do not know who he was. A policeman, or an American agent. But he was armed and we exchanged fire. Samir was killed. I was wounded, but I managed to escape. I thought it best to warn you to advise the others."

"Raffi, what will you do?"

"Nothing. I believe I will die, Rachim. My wound is severe. It will not stop bleeding. I cannot risk a hospital or a doctor. They would ask questions. I will not do anything that might endanger the mission, or my brothers. I will find a quiet place and do what must be done. Our mission in this terrible land must go on."

"It will, my brother."

"I will not leave anything the Yankees can identify us by. That I promise."

"I understand, Raffi, and I honor your name and your sacrifice. God will bless and welcome you."

"Yes. Farewell, Rachim. God is great!"

As Rachim Gazli replaced the receiver, he heard a soft footstep. Glancing up, he saw that Nori Hassad had entered the room.

"Who was that?"

"Raffi."

"Is there a problem?"

Gazli nodded. "Raffi and Samir were discovered in Fallil's apartment. There was an exchange of gunfire and Samir was killed. Raffi avoided capture but he was badly wounded. He will not survive. He has pledged to sacrifice himself to ensure our safety."

Hassad shook his head gently.

"The price is high, Rachim."

"But necessary."

"Yes. Did Raffi identify his attacker?"

"No. He was unknown to them. But not without the skill to defeat Raffi and Samir. I must alert the others to be on their guard."

"Rachim, what about the mission?"

Leaning forward, Gazli stared at the older man for a moment, the expression in his dark eyes frightening to see.

"The mission? The mission goes on, Nori. Nothing else matters. It is our purpose. It is our destiny. Nothing will be allowed to stop it."

Hassad retreated. "I will carry on with all the arrangements," he said quietly.

When he was alone again Gazli sat back, his hand resting on the telephone.

This *was* a setback. Raffi's loss was a blow he felt personally. The man had been more than just one of the Disciples, more than a member of the group. They had been friends for many years, had shared much together during the struggles. Raffi's imminent death would be hard to bear, even though they had all accepted the possibility of death when they undertook the mission. All of them had been aware of the risks they took coming to America, the homeland of the Great Satan, where people were born and bred to slaughter their own in the streets of their sprawling and ugly cities. The Americans lived among squalor and deprivation, party to every perversion open to man. They cheated and lied to each other, and were fed a daily diet of rumor and baseness by the many-tentacled monster of the media. It was the American media that had put forth the terrible story about Ayatollah Khalfi. The twisted untruths about a man of honor and devotion had resulted in Khalfi's death, and for that the Americans would pay.

The Disciples of Khalfi walked as innocents in hell on the streets of America, surrounded on all sides by the enmity of a barren culture, a heartless society of evil. They would bring the cleansing flame of Islam to the diseased Americans.

Gazli knew that Raffi wouldn't be the only one to sacrifice himself during the mission. Others would die. But they all embraced that thought with joy, because in death they became eternal, shedding all earthly pain and suffering to go to God. He would welcome them into his paradise, and the falsity of the living world would be as nothing. Death was simply the rite of passage. The means to an end. The acceptance of

God's all-encompassing glory. Bathed in God's light, they would be sheltered and protected for eternity.

Gazli tapped the telephone with his fingers, his mind working busily ahead.

Who, he wondered, was this killer of his brothers? A policeman? Or an American agent working for the corrupt government? Whoever he was, Gazli gave him credit as a professional, someone who would need to be treated with respect.

He picked up the telephone and punched out the number he wanted. When it was answered he identified himself and spoke urgently.

"Be on your guard. You might have an unfriendly visitor. Perhaps more than one. We have had a problem in New York. Samir is dead, and soon, I believe, Raffi will be. He is badly wounded and will not survive. It is his own choice to protect us."

He listened to the reply.

"We go ahead. As long as any of us survive, we carry on. Has the woman provided any information...? Good. Use whatever she has told you. Send people out. But try to get more from her. If she dies, it will be God's will. Her continued existence is of no consequence. Our need is to locate the rest of the people we seek. Once we have completed our mission, we can leave this accursed country. Do what you have to do, and God be with you."

Gazli leaned back after he had put down the receiver.

So the Americans learned of their presence. How? Where did they get their information?

He acknowledged that the Americans had a far-reaching intelligence network, composed of many sections, and those numerous agencies had eyes and ears all over the world. They bought and sold information like so much salt.

Was there a traitor within the Disciples? Gazli dismissed the thought instantly and with contempt. He would never accept that. The Disciples of Khalfi were bonded by a single purpose: to carry out their mission without concern for their own lives. And none of the Disciples would ever waver from that. His own life meant nothing when placed alongside the dictates of the mission.

He thought about the Disciples setting up the European network. It was to be their base on that vast continent, where they had much work to undertake. From their base in Marseilles they would orchestrate their ongoing campaign in Europe and Britain. Perhaps there had been a leak from Europe, enough for the Americans to connect and send in one of their paid assassins.

Gazli sighed impatiently. It was no help to sit around indulging in speculation. There were many things to do. Plans to make.

He was reminded of Hassad. The man was always on the move, always ready to help and to advise. Hassad was a true disciple of Islam. Perhaps a little weaker than the rest, but that was to be expected from someone who had been forced to live and work in this godless land. Hassad, possibly, had spent too much time in America, but his contribution was invaluable. Through his business enterprises he had gained many contacts and knew the ways of America. His guidance, teaching and organization had helped to pave the way for the others who would follow. So it would only be tolerant to allow him his frailties—as long as they didn't interfere with the mission.

2

After a hard drive through the night, Mack Bolan exited his rental car into a misty Connecticut dawn. Clad in his blacksuit and rigged for war, the Executioner made a recon sweep of the area before closing in on his target.

Stony Man had furnished him with an address to match the telephone number taken from the dead terrorist.

A secluded vacation lodge on the coast, with a view across Long Island Sound, had been rented from a company specializing in holiday retreats. The house was similar to others in the area, in that it stood in solitary isolation. It had been built for privacy and was self-contained, the kind of place ideally suited for a group of people who wanted freedom to come and go without restrictions.

Bolan crouched in the dewy grass, his keen eyes studying the layout. Time, or more precisely the *lack* of it, was forcing his hand. He was making his approach with little knowledge of how many he might be facing. The warrior was also denied any indication of the firepower the opposition might employ.

Blending with the shadows, he examined the outline of the house. Thin light burned behind drawn blinds. Even at his distance from the structure he was able to see thin curls of smoke issuing from the stone chimney. It appeared that someone was awake. A poor sleeper? Or a gunner waiting for him to show up? Bolan hadn't forgotten the wounded terrorist who had given him the slip in New York.

The Executioner's ears picked up on a faint disturbance in the brush close by. It came from his left. He concentrated, and the sound repeated itself. There was no doubt. Someone was moving in his general direction.

Bolan eased the Beretta from its shoulder holster, took off the safety and slid to ground level, waiting, assessing the situation even as it unfolded before him.

Shadows detached from the darkness, moving slowly, but without deliberate intent. Two men were armed with stubby Ingram M-10s fitted with long, heavy MAC suppressors.

Whatever else they were, these people were no vacationers. Not with weaponry like that.

Bolan picked up the murmur of their voices as they eased past his hiding place. The low conversation that reached him was in Farsi.

He waited until the gunners had moved out of earshot, then slid from cover. Keeping low, he cut across the open ground, flattening himself against the side wall of the house. Bolan followed the line of the wall, emerging at the rear of the structure and seeing three cars parked there. Two of them had New York plates. The third was a 4 × 4 Cherokee with local plates.

A half-dressed figure appeared on the stoop, hair and clothing still rumpled from sleep. The guy was attempting to light a cigarette dangling from his mouth, his movements slow as he struggled to drag himself into the new day.

His wandering gaze settled on Mack Bolan as the probing warrior stepped into view from around the corner of the house.

The early riser snapped out of his lethargic state in a split second, turning back to shout over his shoulder, and reached down to snatch up the AK-74 assault rifle leaning against the door frame.

The Executioner took a running leap for cover behind the bulk of the 4 × 4, hitting the soft earth on his shoulder and rolling behind the front wheel.

The harsh rattle of the AK-74 broke the predawn silence. The 4 × 4 rocked as a stream of 5.45 mm slugs raked the body.

The yelling gunner clattered noisily down the steps, skirting the parked vehicles as he tried to locate his target.

Bolan didn't allow him a second chance.

As the guy edged around the rear of the 4 × 4, he was suddenly confronted by the Executioner's black-clad figure. There was a short moment of stillness, then the warrior's right arm snapped around, the 93-R's muzzle lifting fractionally as a triburst drilled 9 mm slugs into the terrorist's skull. His head snapped back, trailing a thin mist of blood. Brain-dead before he hit the ground, the Disciple of Khalfi lost his battle before the war got under way.

The falling numbers were clicking through Bolan's mind as he jammed the Beretta back in leather and ran forward, snatching up the discarded Kalashnikov.

His advantage had gone. Discretion no longer mattered. It was down to pure survival now, a simple choice over who lived and who died.

Movement intruded on the edge of his vision—the pair who had passed Bolan only minutes before. Guns up and ready, they were pounding the earth hard as they raced to join the firefight.

Bolan meet them with his acquired weapon on track. A withering burst from the AK-74 scythed into the terrorist pair. The hollowpoint slugs shredded flesh and bone, organ and sinew. Life erupted from the writhing bodies in bloody gouts, dumping the pair on the ground.

Already turning, Bolan met another Disciple as the man raced from the stoop. He was naked to the waist, black hair flowing behind him. A heavy automatic pistol in his right hand was banging out shot after shot, all directed at the Executioner, all wasted because the shooter was aiming wild. A short burst from the AK-74 punched bloody holes through the gunner's chest, spinning him off balance. He crashed to the ground in a heavy, uncontrolled sprawl.

Bolan kept moving, closing in on the house. He hit the steps and leaped onto the stoop, ducking low as he went in through the door.

He was in the kitchen.

Voices called to each other; footsteps thundered back and forth.

Bolan heard someone approaching the kitchen, and he flattened against the wall, the Kalashnikov pulled tight to his chest.

The armed man who came through the kitchen door hadn't expected the intruder to be inside the house, and his error was costly. Bolan swept the hard stock of the AK-74 in a short, brutal arc that caught the terrorist in the throat. Fatally injured, the Disciple of Khalfi staggered across the kitchen, choking noisily. He fell across the cluttered table, tipping it over as he fell.

By that time the Executioner was through the kitchen door and moving across the expansive living room. Thick rugs were scattered over the polished wood floor. A huge open fireplace dominated one wall, and a wide picture window looked out toward the ocean.

Bolan cast aside the assault rifle and unleathered the Beretta. He moved across the room, aware that the earlier noise had ceased. Silence had cloaked the house again.

He reached the far side of the living room and paused to one side of the door. Beyond lay a spacious lobby that led to the main entrance.

An armed figure was poised by the front door, preparing to open it.

The warrior stepped into view, the 93-R tracking the gunner. A single 3-round burst drilled into the terrorist, punching him to the floor in a lifeless heap.

An uneasy silence settled over the scene.

Bolan prowled the house, searching each room. He found nothing until he opened one door and stood facing a young woman wearing torn, soiled and bloody underclothes. Her face and body were badly bruised and cut. She had split lips, and cigarette burns marred her neck and chest.

For long seconds they stared at each other, then the woman said, "Do you want to kill me, too?"

Bolan shook his head.

"I'm here to to help you," he said, turning toward the living room. The woman followed, her bare feet making soft sounds on the wood floor. When she reached the living room, she went to the long couch that stood against a wall and curled up at one end, her staring eyes on Mack Bolan as he finalized his search.

When he'd finished he crossed to where the woman sat watching him. As he neared her, she cowered, crowding against the end of the couch in sheer terror.

"Please don't let them touch me again."

"Take it easy," Bolan said gently. "I'm not going to let anyone hurt you."

The woman stared at him, fear still bright in her large eyes. She studied him closely, taking in the blacksuit hung with weaponry, and the Beretta, which was still in his hand. Sensing her unease, Bolan stayed back, lowering the weapon to his side.

"I heard shooting. Was that you?"

He nodded. "They weren't the friendliest bunch I've ever met."

"Are they . . . dead?"

"Yeah."

"I suppose that's a sort of good news." She fixed her gaze on Bolan's face. "Are you a cop? FBI? Or just some wacko with a gun?"

"No."

"No what?"

"No to all three."

The woman slumped back against the wall, her slim shoulders dropping as if every last drop of energy had dissipated.

"I don't care who you are as long as you don't start..." Her voice trailed off as she recalled something unpleasant. Her shoulders shook as she began to cry very quietly. Almost as an afterthought she drew her body into a tight ball, pulling her arms close to her head, shutting out the world for a while.

Bolan watched her and realized there was little he could do for her right now. She needed to erase some bad memories, and to do that she had to be given some space. He backed away, holstering the Beretta, and took time to run a quick check on the house, returning to complete his examination of the main room.

There was nothing in it other than the furniture he expected and a scattering of empty soft-drink cans and the remains of leftover food on plates.

Bolan sank into one of the chairs and picked up the telephone. He punched in the number that would eventually connect him with Stony Man Farm.

It was Barbara Price who spoke first.

"Hi, Striker. What's up? Need to talk to Hal?"

"Yeah. And stay on the line. I'll need you to run some checks on calls made from this number."

Brognola came on the line, his voice heavy from lack of sleep.

"Good news or the other kind?"

"The Intel was good. Our friends were here."

"You make hard contact?"

"Yeah. They won't be causing us any more problems. I also found a friendly. A young woman. It appears they'd been giving her a rough ride."

"Is she all right?" Price asked on the other line, her concern showing in her voice.

"Shook up. Some bad bruising. Maybe worse. I haven't quizzed her. She doesn't need that right now. From the way she's been handled I'd guess they were trying to get information out of her."

"Any ideas?"

"She's still a little upset. I'll talk to her once she's settled. We need a clean-up team out here and someone to look after the girl."

"I'll get on it," Price said.

"Striker, what do you make of it all?" Brognola asked.

"Local base, I'd say. Isolated so they wouldn't be noticed. But there's something missing. I don't think the top man was here. There's no arms stash, no explosives. This isn't the operations center."

"You didn't get them all, you know!"

Bolan turned as the woman spoke.

She had crossed the room to stand next to him, her arms crossed over her chest.

"All who?"

"The men here."

"How do you know?"

"There were telephone calls earlier. Before you arrived. After that they all had some kind of conference. I couldn't understand what it was about because they spoke in—I don't know, Farsi, I guess. Then three of them did some packing and left."

Bolan had been holding the telephone toward the woman.

"You get that?" he asked.

"Yeah," Brognola growled.

"But we don't know where they headed," Bolan added.

"Yes we do," the woman said.

Bolan watched her. Despite her red-rimmed eyes she appeared to be back in control of her emotions. She moved to the chair across from Bolan and sat.

"I'm Eve Jordan. I have a brother called Harry. It's Harry these people are after. They want to kill him. Something to do with a news story about one of those Iranian ayatollahs that he worked on when he was with the NewsForce team. Two days ago they grabbed me off the street and brought me here. They can't find Harry now that he's left the team. They did those things to me to make me talk. I tried to hold out, but I was scared. I thought I was going to die. I think I might have let something slip when they were really hurting me. It could be enough for them to track Harry down."

"Eve, listen to me," Bolan said. "You're right about these people. They want to kill everyone who was involved in that news story. Do you remember Ras Fallil?

Jordan nodded.

"I knew him very well. He was good friend. A nice person."

"He was murdered earlier today in New York. When I went to his apartment to check things out, there were two men searching it. One died and one escaped after I wounded him. That was probably why the people here decided to move on your brother. Now I need to know where Harry is. If I can get to him soon, I might be in time to stop these people from killing him, too.''

The woman digested Bolan's information calmly, then said, ''I can tell you exactly where he is. Please, you've got to save him. Don't let those men kill my brother.''

3

Bolan ran from the house to where Jack Grimaldi had just touched down on the windswept shore in Dragon Slayer, the sleek black combat helicopter from Stony Man. The chopper was one of a kind, designed and commissioned by the Sensitive Operations Group, and was used as a Stony Man operations backup. Dragon Slayer was equipped with an array of weaponry and electronics that couldn't be bought. Everything on the machine had been specially designed and built for her alone. The aircraft was a combat pilot's dream.

As Bolan settled in the body-form seat alongside Grimaldi, the flier gave him a nod, then powered the chopper off the ground. Bolan buckled himself in as the access hatch beside him locked shut with a thump of hydraulics.

Grimaldi angled the helicopter away from the house, following the contours of the coast for a while, before turning inland and heading west. Setting the course by punching in coordinates on the inboard computer system, the Stony Man pilot waited as the screen re-formed itself and brought up a fresh display. Then he keyed in an acceptance code.

Glancing across at Bolan, he asked, "How's it going, Sarge?"

"As ever," the Executioner replied, harnessing himself in for the long flight.

Dawn was paling the night sky as Dragon Slayer reached altitude and leveled out. Grimaldi raised the power, the chopper's twin turboshaft engines—each rated at 1,690 shaft horsepower—hurling the craft across the empty sky. The murmuring radio suddenly burst into life as they sped from one airspace jurisdiction to another. Grimaldi responded to requests for ID, referring the callers to the clearance codes assigned to Dragon Slayer. Once these had been verified, the pilot was given the all clear and sent on his way without hindrance.

Beside the flier, Mack Bolan caught some rest. He used this brief stretch of calm to sleep, knowing that once they reached their destination he would get little opportunity to recharge his batteries. Sleep would be at the lower end of his list of priorities. Bolan had been a combat soldier all his adult life, in one form or another, and he still retained the fighting man's ability to snatch rest between engagements. There was little else to do. Between takeoff and landing he was in Jack Grimaldi's capable hands. The Stony Man pilot didn't need anyone holding his hand. He knew exactly where he was going and how to get there.

Grimaldi allowed Bolan to sleep. He knew that the man, as usual, would have been pushing himself to the limit. The warrior's life seemed to be permanently on full throttle. He was constantly on the go, moving from mission to mission with little pause in between. The wonder was that he seldom showed any signs of slowing down. In fact, he appeared to thrive on the challenges his ongoing war threw his way. It was often left to others to provide him with the opportunity to recuperate.

They were well into the morning by the time Grimaldi brought the helicopter to earth in a quiet corner of a small private airfield near Knoxville, Tennessee. As the rotors slowed and the engines wound down, the pilot picked up the handset and spoke to Hal Brognola back at Stony Man.

"You want to speak to Striker?" the flier asked.

"Yeah," Brognola said.

Grimaldi turned to wake Bolan and found him already alert, reaching out to take the handset.

"Hal, you have any luck with that name I passed along?"

"Some," the big Fed said. "Aaron is still digging. He'll come up with the goods."

"How about Eve Jordan?"

"She's in safe hands, hospitalized and under protection. We'll see she gets the best."

"I'm sure she'll settle for having her brother back alive," Bolan said.

"Did Jack bring you everything you need?"

"Yeah. I'm moving out now. Keep Jack up-to-date."

"Will do, Striker."

Bolan eased out of the seat and into the passenger compartment to find two carryalls, one holding weapons and equipment, the other street clothing. The warrior pulled pants and shirt over his blacksuit, then donned a leather jacket. His combat harness went into the weapons carryall. A pocket in the jacket contained a wallet, which held credit cards, cash and a driver's license.

"I'll pick up a cab into town," Bolan said, "then hire a car and go after Harry Jordan."

Grimaldi nodded. He handed the Executioner a compact package that contained a powerful transceiver.

"She's all powered up. Got a good range and she's set to my frequency. Keep in touch when you head out so I can track you. If we can keep in range and you call for the cavalry, don't be surprised if I come over the hill."

Bolan packed the radio in his carryall.

"Thanks, Jack."

"Watch your back, pal."

The warrior waved a hand in farewell as he exited the helicopter and crossed to the airfield's administration building. Inside he found a sleepy manager reading an early edition of the local newspaper.

"Can I call a cab from here?"

The man lowered his paper and peered at Bolan over the rims of his eyeglasses.

"You need a ride to town?"

"Yeah."

"Hold on, mister."

The man laid down his paper and strolled to a door. Opening it, he leaned out and yelled to someone. A lean figure dressed in faded denims and a baseball cap followed the manager back to his counter.

"Eddie, here, is just going back into town. He brings out the mail and newspapers every morning. Be glad of the company."

"No trouble?" Bolan asked.

Eddie shook his head. Turning on his heel, he made his way out of the building.

"There you go," the manager said.

"Thanks," Bolan replied. "I guess Eddie's not the talkative kind."

The manager smiled. "You could say."

A battered, dusty Dodge pickup was parked outside. It looked like something off the cover of *Saturday Evening Post,* and Eddie, leaning against the open door, could have been a Rockwell model.

Bolan walked around and climbed in, placing his carryall on the floor between his feet.

Tipping his cap to the back of his head, Eddie pulled his door shut. He turned the key, and the Dodge's engine caught instantly, turning over with well-oiled smoothness. Eddie eased it into gear and the pickup rolled from the curb with barely a murmur.

"Nice," Bolan commented.

"She's beautiful." Eddie handled the purring engine with reverence. "Been in the family since the late fifties. My grandpa bought her new. Never seen the inside of a service shop. Always been looked after by the family. Original engine is under that hood, mister. Outlast any of those damn Japanese things they chase around in today."

Bolan didn't doubt it.

"You know this area well?" the warrior asked.

"Sure. Hey, let me guess. You wouldn't want to know the quickest way up to the bluffs over by the O & W Bridge?"

Bolan tensed, though he didn't allow it to show on his face.

"Is it becoming popular, Eddie?"

The man laughed. "Yeah. Three guys asked me this morning. Real early. They were in town when I was loading up over to the store. They just come in from the airfield and hired themselves a 4 × 4. Said they were on vacation and come to look at the wilderness. Foreign-looking fellers, you know. Dark. Black hair.'' He paused to glance across at Bolan. "You a cop?"

"Do I look like one?"

Eddie's laugh was sharp, nervous, which was often the reaction when ordinary citizens believed they were in the presence of a law officer.

"Damn right you do."

Bolan fished out the leather wallet he carried for a situation like this. It contained a Justice Department special-agent badge and a printed ID, made out in the name Mike Blanski. Hal Brognola had provided the badge, aware that it could open doors that might otherwise be shut to his covert SOG operatives.

Eddie stared at the badge, then at Bolan, and the look in his eyes revealed that he was impressed.

"Not a cop, Eddie. But I am looking for someone and I think you can help me."

"Don't cost to ask."

"The three men you described aren't vacationers. They're foreign nationals, in the U.S. illegally. They came here looking for a man by the name of Harry Jordan. He came here to film the wildlife up on the bluffs. Those men mean him harm, and I have to get to Harry before they do."

"Jordan turned up about a week back and took himself up into the wilderness. Said he needed it real peaceful so he could film the wildlife without disturbing them. Real nice feller. Now who would want to hurt him, Mr. Blanski?"

"Some people who didn't like something he filmed for a television program. The kind who take things personally. Harry did nothing wrong, but these people don't see it that way. I don't intend to let them harm him."

Eddie pondered Bolan's words. He leaned into the steering wheel and trod down hard on the gas pedal, sending the Dodge speeding along the tarmac road.

Ten minutes later they were rolling onto the lot of a local car-rental agency. Eddie braked in front of the office.

"Hey, Pete, get out here. Man needs a set of wheels right fast, you hear."

Pete organized Bolan's vehicle in record time. It was a chunky Ford 4 × 4, slightly battered, but the best on the lot, according to Eddie.

"She'll take you up the side of a mountain without stalling," he said, watching Bolan transfer his bags. "Hey, you sure you don't want me to let the sheriff know?"

Bolan shook his head. "Thanks, but no. The fewer people in on this, Eddie, the better. The last thing I want are sirens and flashing lights all over. I need to reach Harry Jordan ahead of those guys if I can. If they figure we're on to them, they'll be harder to deal with."

"Put it that way, I guess you're right. Sheriff Loomis is a nice feller, but he does prefer to do everything with a circus in tow, if you know what I mean."

Bolan slipped behind the seat and put the Ford in gear. "I appreciate your help, Eddie."

Eddie grinned. "Ain't every day I get to help on something like this, Mr. Blanski. Now you remember what I told you. Once you cross the bridge, you follow the old trail. She may be rough, but she'll get you to where Harry Jordan is right quick.''

Pushing on the gas pedal, Bolan swung the Ford off the lot and pushed it back along the highway, searching for the turnoff that would shortcut the ride to the O & W Bridge. The turnoff showed up exactly two miles later.

Bolan wrenched the wheel, and the solid 4×4 bounced from the tarmac onto the dusty track. Shortly he returned to the road that brought him to the old bridge that crossed the Cumberland River just below the O & W Rapids. Across the bridge, he headed along the winding trail that pushed deep into the timbered bluffs.

A mile in and he spotted the narrow, rutted trail that angled off from the road, and swung the 4×4 in a hard right curve. As the trail vanished in the trees ahead of him, Bolan felt low branches slap against the roof and overhangs brush the side windows. The high canopy formed by the close-knit branches cut out the daylight. Near the forest floor dark shadows spread out across the rutted trail. A thin film of raised dust hung in the air behind the Ford 4×4 as Bolan pushed deeper into the forest, following the directions Eddie had furnished.

Minutes later he crossed the shallow creek he had been told to watch out for. The trail forked on the opposite side, and Bolan took the left branch, almost immediately seeing that the trail started to climb ahead of him.

The forest thinned out now, the brightening day filling the world with warm light. A few miles on, Bolan saw the buff rock formations through the thinning tree line. The trail climbed in earnest now, with rocky foothills developing as the vehicle traveled higher. Bolan found he was having to slow his pace. Although the trail was well defined, sections of it skirted steep drops, with rising rock faces on one side and nothing on the other. If he lost control of the vehicle, he might plummet down the jagged, rocky slopes.

According to his watch, Bolan had been driving for two hours, almost to the minute, and was not far off the time Eddie had predicted. The trail rounded a curve, and in front of Bolan was a wide plateau, its top thick with hardwood timber. He followed the trail around the edge until he recognized the bubbling spring that fed water into a deep rock pan and the stream that ran out on the far side. The warrior drew the Ford to a stop and climbed out, stretching his legs and breathing in the fresh air. At any time but this he might have relaxed and enjoyed the natural beauty of the area. Now he was on a trip to save a man's life, and everyday pursuits had to be put aside.

Bolan removed his outer clothing and armed himself, checking the Beretta and the massive Desert Eagle. He checked his position, pinpointing the landmarks Eddie had given him. Knowing where he had to go, the Executioner slipped behind the wheel and moved off again, feeling the surge of power from the Ford as he pushed down on the gas pedal.

He reached trail's end fifteen minutes later, after negotiating long stretches of crumbling track, the Ford edging its way slowly across crumbling shale and broken earth. The sun was high now, with a sky empty of cloud. The air was virtually still. The occasional breeze blowing across the bluffs was warm and dry, and the temperature was still rising.

Reversing the 4×4 into the cover of a rocky overhang, Bolan cut the engine, grabbed the carryall and opened it. He placed a 9 mm Uzi on the seat beside him and drew out the filled magazines. One went into the Uzi, the others were stowed in the ammo pouches on his combat harness. Additional clips for the Beretta and the Desert Eagle were also placed in pouches, and he slid a combat knife into the sheath on his belt.

The Executioner exited the Ford and made his way along the narrowing trail that wound up the side of the bluff. In places it was no more than a foot wide, the earth underfoot loose and liable to collapse when he placed his weight on it. Bolan moved as fast as he dared, conscious all the time that time wasn't on his side. The numbers were falling, and the enemy was closing in.

Finally reaching the next level plateau, and aware that he was very close to Harry Jordan's location, Bolan pushed his way through the tangled undergrowth and stands of timber.

He leaned forward to push low-hanging branches out of his way, but something made him pause, his head coming up as his nostrils caught an unusual scent.

The smell of exhaust smoke.

Bolan grabbed for the Uzi, pulling it around so that the weapon slipped easily into his waiting hands.

His eyes searched the area and caught sight of dark painted metal shielded by greenery. It was a Toyota off-road vehicle, the type Eddie had described to him. The trio had made good time.

A twig cracked to the warrior's left as a careless foot settled over it.

Bolan dropped to a crouch, searching, the Uzi following his gaze.

He spotted a lean figure clad in light clothing who had dark skin and thick, black hair. He was carrying a stubby Ingram MAC-10.

The gunner moved carefully, checking out the way ahead, his head moving from side to side, eyes staring fiercely from a taut, angry face.

Then the man's head snapped around, his eyes seeming to lock on to Bolan's place of concealment. He held his gaze, the subgun sweeping around.

Without a moment's hesitation the guy opened fire, raking the foliage with a deadly stream of slugs that ripped leaves and twigs to shreds, the burst aimed directly at Mack Bolan.

4

Shredded foliage dropped over Bolan like green snow. Above the ugly crackle of the MAC-10 he heard the triggerman yelling. The words were in Farsi, but Bolan caught the urgency in the tone and knew the gunner was calling for his partners. It was time for a temporary retreat.

Staying low, Bolan wriggled backward. The moment he was clear of the firezone, he twisted and rolled, still aware of the terrorist's closeness. The hit man was already committing himself to a fatal move. Instead of waiting for his backup to join him, he had plunged into the dense undergrowth, searching for Bolan.

The Executioner obliged. But his introduction was by way of the Uzi. Up on one knee, Bolan pushed aside the greenery with the Uzi's barrel, and the moment he had the terrorist in his sights he stroked the subgun's trigger. A stream of hot 9 mm slugs caught the advancing gunner at knee level, pitching him to the forest floor where he lay moaning, his hands scrabbling for the Ingram that had slipped from his fingers. Pulling the weapon to him, the Disciple of Khalfi shoved himself into a sitting position, peering around as he tried to locate his attacker.

And found him.

The Executioner faced his enemy across fifteen feet, his face expressionless as he tracked the Uzi in on target. He touched the trigger a second before the terrorist fired his own weapon. The Ingram arced skyward as the terrorist toppled over on his back, his chest ravaged by the Uzi's second burst. The dying man uttered final words of prayer as his life ebbed away, his blood soaking into the rich forest floor. His part in the great mission to America was ended, and he would never know if it succeeded or not.

Turning quickly, Bolan melted into the surrounding forest, making a wide circle of the area. Now that his presence was known and presented a threat to the attempt on Harry Jordan's life, the terrorists would concentrate on their target. Nothing else would matter. Jordan's death would be the sole driving source behind everything they did from now on. Bolan had to assume the same objective—though his motivation was to save Jordan, to keep him alive.

Barely making a sound, his passing nothing more than a fleeting shadow, Bolan sprinted through the forest. His senses were concentrated on the task at hand, which was to reach Jordan before the Disciples of Khalfi.

He wasn't going to have a second chance. The moment Jordan came under the terrorists' sights, they would open fire. The unsuspecting target would probably die without even knowing who had pulled the trigger or why they had done it.

Somewhere in the distance Bolan picked up the beat of a revving engine. It was possible the Disciples were trying to reach Jordan in their vehicle. With Bolan on the scene, the terrorists would want to gain every second. So they had calculated the risk of warning Jordan by using their vehicle to get them to him before Bolan.

The strategy might have worked if they had been up against a lesser man. The knowledge that the terrorists were possibly gaining ground only spurred the warrior on. He cut off at an angle, still keeping the mental picture of the area in his mind. Eddie had described the location down to the last detail, allowing Bolan an insight into the terrain that was most likely denied the terrorists. When he was confronted by a wide stream, he knew he was getting really close. Splashing through it, the warrior powered himself up a high, steep slope, digging in his booted feet until the muscles in his legs screamed for relief. He ignored the brutal pain, pushing harder until he was able to scramble over the crest of the slope. He paused for scant seconds, orientating himself. Off to his left an outcropping marked the extremes of Jordan's filming ground. Within the rocks and tangled brush the man was shooting his film, probably unaware of the impending drama building up to a climax.

The roar of the terrorists' 4 × 4 increased. As Bolan turned, he saw the vehicle lurch over the rim of the slope yards to his right. It crashed down on the ground, raising dust. The heavy tires spun and slipped as the driver pushed the pedal to the floor, gravel flying in all directions. For a moment it looked as if the 4 × 4 wouldn't make it. But then it burst over the rim, bouncing and slithering as it came down on all four wheels.

The passenger door flew open and a man leaned out, cradling a Heckler & Koch MP-5 in his right arm, the stock jammed against his body. He fired a long burst of 9 mm slugs in Bolan's direction, the shots falling short only by inches.

Bolan half turned, bringing the muzzle of the Uzi into line. He triggered a volley that chewed at the 4×4's grille, puncturing the water jacket behind. Steam burst from the holes. The driver ignored the explosion of steam and persisted with his high revs, the 4×4 slithering toward the Executioner.

The warrior dug in his heels, turning aside from the looming bulk of the heavy vehicle. He nearly made it. When almost clear, he felt the rear corner of the body brush him, the force of the impact enough to pick Bolan off his feet and hurl him several yards. He relaxed his muscles the instant before he hit the ground, tucking his head to his chest and rolling to lessen the impact. He stopped inches from the edge of the bluff, with the steep slope falling away. Disturbed stones rattled down the incline, raising dust in their wake.

Gathering his legs under him, the warrior pushed upright, the Uzi up and tracking as he heard a wild scream of defiance.

The terrorist with the H&K subgun had leaped from the 4×4 and was racing in Bolan's direction, triggering the weapon on the move. The expended slugs chewed the earth short of the Executioner.

The terrorist screamed and yelled as he advanced, his passion exploding in a torrent of words.

Bolan held his fire for heart-pounding seconds, determined not to allow panic to dictate his actions. Only when he had the gunner fully in his sights did he trigger the Uzi.

An instant before the subgun spit flame, one of the terrorist's bullets clipped Bolan's left side, just above his waist. The Executioner felt the lance of pain, immediately followed by a rush of hot blood that soaked through his blacksuit. His grip on the Uzi remained constant, and his pull on the trigger followed through.

The terrorist was drilled through the chest by a concentrated burst of 9 mm slugs. He was pushed off course by the impact, his limbs losing coordination. He stumbled and went down on his knees, the muzzle of his weapon dropping to the ground and scoring a furrow in the earth. Already out of the fight, the terrorist crashed facedown, his body spasming as his ravaged nervous system responded to the shock of the bullets.

A heavy crash of sound alerted Bolan. He stepped past the dead gunner, replacing the spent magazine of the Uzi with a fresh one. Cocking the weapon, he moved on across the bluff, checking the way ahead.

The 4×4 had come to a halt against an outcropping. The driver's door hung open, the seat empty.

Bolan moved on past the vehicle, his eyes searching the jumble of rock and brush.

Somewhere ahead he picked up a rattle of sound—the patter of disturbed stone. He located the source of the noise and spotted a faint haze of dust in the air ahead of him, and higher up.

Almost in the same instant a figure appeared on a narrow ledge even higher up the rocky escarpment. The man was clad in outdoor clothing and carried an assortment of camera equipment. He stared about him, obviously startled by the disturbance.

His angry yell reached Bolan before the Executioner could give his own warning.

The man's exclamation was punctuated by the spiteful crack of a high-powered rifle. The bullet struck rock inches from his left shoulder.

"Find cover, Jordan! Now!"

To his credit Harry Jordan reacted swiftly, dropping from sight instantly.

Sunlight glinted on the moving barrel of a rifle as it tracked in on Bolan. He twisted to one side, hearing the crack of the weapon. The bullet scored a white flash on the rock where the warrior had been standing.

Bolan circled the boulder that was providing cover and emerged on the far side, ducking low as he sprinted for the slope before him. As he ran he scanned the heights above, searching for the hidden rifleman.

The terrorist broke cover, climbing with surprising agility. Despite Bolan's presence, he seemed determined to reach Jordan and carry out the execution.

Reaching a wide expanse of flat rock, the Executioner pushed forward, concentrating on the task ahead and trying to ignore the burn of pain from his side. He kept the moving terrorist in sight.

The hardman halted, raising the rifle to his shoulder, aiming at something below him, out of Bolan's sight.

The warrior raised the Uzi and triggered a burst that fell short, but which laid a trail of slugs close enough to the terrorist to break his concentration. He sidestepped as stone chips struck his legs, turning to face his attacker.

The hardman got off a shot, the bullet whipping close enough to Bolan to make him cautious. The terrorist adjusted his aim hastily and fired again.

The Executioner had already dropped to a crouch, angling the Uzi up at the lean figure outlined against the backdrop of the empty sky. His finger stroked the trigger and laid a destructive stream of 9 mm slugs in the terrorist's torso, flinging him back off the edge of the rock he was perched on. The gunner gave a startled cry and vanished from Bolan's sight.

"I HAD A FEELING something like this might happen when we started getting those damn threats," Harry Jordan said. "Letters, the odd telephone call, all saying the same thing. That we were all going to pay for what we'd done to Khalfi. None of the others paid any attention to it except me and Fallil. In the end I'd had enough. Maybe I'm not as committed as the others. I didn't need the hassle. I figured it was time to move on, do something else. I'd been wanting to come out here and make my own film for some time, so I upped and quit, got myself organized and came out here a couple of weeks back. I guess I was fooling myself into believing I could lose those guys if I came out here and tried to forget them. I should have known better."

Bolan sighed. There was no way he could wrap this up nicely.

"Harry, they killed Ras Fallil yesterday. His body was found in his car in New York."

Jordan stared out beyond the warrior, his eyes unashamedly glistening with tears. "God damn it," he said tautly. "Not Ras. Those bastards."

"I'm sorry," Bolan said. "We only picked up on this yesterday. By the time I got to the city Fallil was already dead. I ran into a couple of the Disciples at his apartment and got the location of the place they were using up in Connecticut."

"And?"

"Closed it down."

"How did you find me so quick?"

"Eve told me where you were."

Jordan looked at Bolan, his eyes suddenly sharp, penetrating.

"You've involved Eve?"

"She was already involved. They had her at the house in Maine. They made her tell them where you were."

"God Almighty. Is she hurt? Did they...?"

"She's fine, Harry. They used some force to make her talk, but she's okay now. And she's safe. They can't get to her."

"This is getting worse. It's like a nightmare. Now my sister is caught up in it. I wish I'd never been involved with that damned film."

Jordan scrubbed his hands through his hair, staring around with the look of a man who wasn't sure which way was up any longer.

"Your timing was pretty good," Bolan said. "Only these guys were determined to find you."

"My gut feeling was right, though," Jordan stated. "I knew something bad would come from it all along. Hell, we should have known better. Too many people have found themselves on the wrong side of these fundamentalists.''

Bolan nodded. He knew exactly what Jordan was saying.

''One thing I have learned about them. They don't mess around. Everything is for real. They make a commitment, and when they do they don't quit until you are dead—or they are. Problem is, once you step over the line with these guys, there's no walking away. It doesn't do any good to say you're sorry, and there's no point trying to reason with them. They can't hear you. They don't forgive, or forget. And they never let go.''

He stared around the timbered landscape, regret in his face.

''Tell me, what was I supposed to do? Rent a billboard in Times Square and tell them where I was? 'Sorry, guys, I did you wrong so I'm going to stand here until you come and get me.' Shoot myself? Take a fast jet to Iran and hand myself over? We did our job, that's all. Now it looks like I'll be dodging those bastards the rest of my life. Well, the hell with them. I might be scared, but I'm not going into hiding. This is my damn country, not theirs, and they don't have the right to do what they want.''

Jordan slumped against an outcropping, spent from his outburst. He looked up at Bolan, almost apologetic.

''I guess I had my say. Now I feel like an idiot.''

''No reason why you should,'' Bolan told him. ''You're right. Whatever grievance these Disciples have, it doesn't open the door to wholesale murder. If they have a complaint, it should be dealt with through the proper channels. Not by sending in assassination teams to torture and kill.''

"So where do we go from here?''

"Right now I take you back with me. Get you reunited with your sister in protective custody until this terrorist group has been dealt with. After that you can decide how you want to play it.''

"The answer to that is, I want to get on with my life. I'll get used to looking over my shoulder if that's what it takes. But I won't play hide-and-seek with those people. If they want me, I won't be hard to find.''

"You keep thinking like that, and we'll beat them. It's the only way.''

THERE WAS A CALL from Stony Man waiting for Bolan when he returned to Grimaldi and the helicopter.

He took the handset the pilot passed to him and carried on the conversation while Grimaldi cleaned and bandaged the bullet gouge he'd received during the firefight with the terrorists.

"Striker, go ahead.''

"Hey, big guy," Aaron Kurtzman's voice boomed down the line. "I've got some locations for you.''

"I'm listening.''

"There were two numbers they called from the house in Connecticut. One was a ski lodge up near Aspen, Colorado, owned by a guy named Nori Hassad. The other was a restaurant in Chicago's South Side.''

"Come on, Bear, give. I can tell you've got something juicy in there.''

Kurtzman chuckled. "Hell, Striker, let me have a little fun. You listening . . . ? Okay. I ran some checks on the restaurant. Had to do some sneaking around, but guess what I found?"

"I give up," Bolan said.

"When you come to the end of the line, the restaurant is owned by the same guy who runs the ski lodge. Nori Hassad."

5

There was a growing sense of urgency driving him, something niggling at the back of his mind that was trying to warn him time was slipping away too quickly. That he needed to step up the pace before matters got beyond his control.

Chicago then.

Bolan stood in the latticework shadows beneath the El, only his eyes moving as he watched the comings and goings at the restaurant across the way.

It had been two hours of nothing but customers visiting the place, and they were few on this cold, wet night. Yet he still felt there was more going on behind the facade of the eating establishment than the menu might show.

He hadn't failed to notice the man who kept emerging from the side door in the adjoining alley. Each time the guy showed, he paced to the mouth of the alley and peered up and down the street, checking his watch frequently before going back inside. His agitation aroused Bolan's interest.

Something or someone was expected at the restaurant. The Executioner didn't believe it to be anything as innocent as a late delivery of bread rolls.

At 10:30 p.m. the last of the customers were seen off the premises. The front door was locked, and the sign turned to Closed before the main lights were extinguished.

Bolan continued to wait. He was cold, there was no denying that, but he pushed the physical discomfort aside and concentrated on watching the restaurant. He hunched deeper into the leather jacket, pulling the collar tight around his neck. He wore street clothes, with the Beretta 93-R snug in shoulder leather and spare clips for the handgun resting in a closed inner pocket. He had decided against carrying too much armament on this trip. If things turned hard inside the restaurant, or on the street, with the possibility of civilians around, he didn't need the problem of a subgun or machine pistol spraying bullets indiscriminately. Innocent people were too often caught up in violent situations, and Bolan didn't want to be responsible for any of them being hurt by his own fire. At least with the Beretta he had more control over his shots.

His rental car was parked against the curb around the corner in a nonrestricted zone, and providing it wasn't hijacked by local car thieves, it would provide him with a quick getaway.

According to Kurtzman's Intel, the restaurant was run by a couple of Lebanese brothers who had been in the country for more than five years. They had bought the restaurant with a cash payment and had been open for business within a month. The vendor had been glad to accept cash with no questions. He had been trying to sell the place for two years and was relieved to get it off his hands. Deeper digging by the Bear, who had the ability to dredge up information that no one else dreamed existed, had unearthed a connection between the brothers and Nori Hassad. This had been back in Toronto, Canada, roughly two years previous. Even then Hassad had been tied in with the fringes of the Shiite fundamentalists. Nothing anyone could prove in a court of law, but as Kurtzman followed the thin line of inquiry, his computers plucked out strands of information that began to build a wider picture involving Nori Hassad.

He was a businessman. His affiliation aside, he was an entrepreneur, and that tied him into the business community worldwide. It followed that he was involved in banking procedures when it came to money matters. To present himself as a legitimate financier, Hassad had to follow accepted practice. He couldn't conduct his enterprises bankrolled by a wad of money in his hip pocket. Not for his regular transactions. So his up-front dealings were a matter of record, on the data bases of institutions that reached as far as London, Tokyo and a number of American banks. Hassad was no man's fool. He had created a series of companies that were nothing more than covers for his backdoor dealings.

That was nothing new to Aaron Kurtzman, and he got a buzz from taking the thinnest of leads and tracing them back through the maze of financial chicanery until he had a definite link to his main thread. Kurtzman, dedicated and artful in the extreme, weaved his way back and forth between phony companies set up in the Bahamas and banks on three continents, examining fund shuffling and cash payments, until he had established that Hassad not only bankrolled the Lebanese restaurant, but also appeared to be financing a number of other organizations linked to the fundamentalist cause. It was a complicated web of interactive dealings, but the bottom line was clear and well defined—Nori Hassad was a loyal member of the cause.

His financial empire was providing money and support for the fundamentalists both within the U.S. and in Europe. The Chicago restaurant was in the middle of the maze, its full role uncertain but certainly linked to the cause.

Which brought Mack Bolan, the Executioner, to his lonely vigil on a cold Chicago night, with the promise of warming things up for the Disciples.

At 10:50 p.m. an unmarked panel truck rolled along the street. It drew to a halt by the restaurant, then reversed into the alley beside the building. Bolan watched as the driver and his companion climbed out, walked to the rear of the vehicle and opened the door. While one man climbed inside, the other tapped on the restaurant's side door. It was opened, and several men stepped into the alley. In a matter of minutes a number of boxes and wooden cases were transferred from the truck to the restaurant.

The two men returned to the vehicle, each carrying an aluminum case. Bolan memorized the license plates as the truck rolled out of the alley and vanished along the street.

Soon after, three men left the restaurant and walked away along the deserted street.

The moment the door closed behind the remaining men, the warrior crossed the street and entered the alley. He paused to check out the area, easing the Beretta from its holster. Illuminated by a dull lamp over the restaurant's side door, the alley was shadowed and silent. Steam issued from a vent in the grimy wall, drifting away in the cool breeze wafting the alley's length.

Bolan reached the door without challenge. Whatever else they were up to, standing guard over their domain didn't rate high on the opposition's list. He checked the door, which was locked. That didn't surprise him. He moved along the alley until he spotted a window with the upper section open. Bolan located a trash can, stood on the lid and reached up to free the catch on the frame. He eased the window open and peered inside.

The restaurant kitchen spread out before him. The place was in darkness except for two low-wattage bulbs glowing over one of the stoves. The aroma of rich coffee reached Bolan's nostrils and made his stomach growl with hunger. Checking to make sure the kitchen was deserted, the warrior climbed inside, stepping to the floor via the stainless-steel sink that was flush to the wall. He closed the window behind him in case someone did some checking.

The kitchen opened up into the restaurant through swing doors. The warrior passed under an archway and traveled along a short corridor. Light seeped onto the carpet from the bottom of a door several yards distant, and Bolan could make out the soft murmur of voices.

A creak of sound made the Executioner turn, the Beretta up and tracking. The corridor was empty, but he heard other sounds, realizing in a second that they were coming from somewhere below him.

Bolan backtracked and spotted the recessed door farther along the corridor. It stood partway open, and light reached up the flight of steps that led into the basement area. The warrior started down the steps, stopping at the point where they angled to the right. He flattened himself against the wall and listened to the conversations coming from below.

Several people were speaking in Farsi, the conversation accompanied by the sound of feverish activity. Someone, Bolan decided, was busy.

Doing what?

He was about to descend farther when he picked up the merest whisper of shoe leather on one of the steps behind him. The Executioner twisted his upper body, bringing the 93-R to bear, and spotted a lean figure outlined against the open doorway.

The dull gleam of a matt-black subgun angled down at Bolan.

Acting out of pure instinct, the Executioner dropped flat on the steps, thrusting the Beretta out and up.

The subdued hiss of suppressed slugs burned the air. They impacted against the stone wall, gouging dime-sized chips that peppered the Executioner.

He returned fire, his precisely aimed 3-round burst chopping through his adversary's throat and emerging from the base of his skull.

As the gunner fell backward Bolan pushed himself to his feet. About to head for the door, he hesitated, warned by some inner sense. A second gunner appeared, shoving aside his mortally wounded companion. He leaned over the top step and opened fire without a moment's hesitation.

Bolan was forced to haul himself back out of the way as a sustained burst blanketed the area with deadly fire. His action caused the warrior to topple backward. He lost his balance and fell against the opposite wall, then pitched headfirst down the steps.

Bolan tucked in his head and shoulders and pulled in the Beretta, shielding it with his body as he rolled and twisted down the steps. He hit bottom with a thump, aware of frantic yelling all around him.

Knowing full well that his next moments could be his last, Bolan took control of the situation. Ignoring the bruises and grazes he had suffered, he rolled to his feet, the Beretta tracking in as he scanned the basement.

His sudden appearance had taken the occupants by surprise. It was likely to be a short reprise, Bolan realized as he rose to his feet, one that would offer the best advantage to the person who responded fastest.

Three people were in the basement.

The Executioner had already located one armed hardman on the far side of the basement. He was reacting with almost comical slowness, and as his distant gaze locked with the Executioner's, the Beretta 93-R spoke decisively. The triburst ended the gunner's life, taking him out of play forever.

One of the surviving men, his dark hair flying, lunged forward and made a grab for a heavy autopistol lying on the workbench he'd been at. His fingers barely had time to close over the butt before Bolan triggered the Beretta again, drilling a 3-round burst into his temple. The impact of the 9 mm slugs snapped the terrorist's head back, and a dark spray of blood misted out from the open wounds. He crashed backward onto the concrete floor, his spine arching in a final protest against the all too brief burst of pain.

Bolan heard footsteps coming down the basement steps. He sidestepped behind the slim cover of a nearby brick wall, his eyes picking out the movement of the third terrorist as the man bent, then straightened. He held an automatic shotgun and started triggering the weapon the moment he pulled it above the level of the workbench, sending blasts of buckshot in the Executioner's general direction. The spread peppered the wall to Bolan's left, some of it missing the edge of the wall and hammering into the wall at the back of the steps.

The loose shot made the man on the steps pause—only for a few seconds, but long enough for Bolan to track the Beretta two-fisted at the shotgunner, hold, then loose off a burst that shredded the hardman's throat and slammed him to the floor, choking on his own blood.

Dropping the dry clip from the Beretta, Bolan then rammed home a fresh one. Cocking the 93-R, he turned toward the steps, forcing the action, and caught the gunner as he began his descent again.

The terrorist, his bearded face taut with a mixture of anger and determination, shouted in rage as Bolan appeared before him. He dropped the muzzle of the Ingram MAC-10, his finger tightening against the trigger. Before the gunner could complete the action, he felt a hammer blow in his chest that stopped him in his tracks. His breathing became labored and the shadowed steps became completely dark. He succumbed to the prevailing void, unaware of his own death fall as he crashed to the bottom of the steps.

Mounting the steps, the Executioner paused by the door, ears straining to pick up any sounds. He heard nothing, and after a brief pause he ventured into the corridor. His senses told him he was alone in the place, but he wasn't foolish enough to be totally secure until he had made a thorough search of the building, checking every room. Only when he was satisfied that the place was secure did Bolan return to the basement.

The workbench attracted his attention, and he wasn't surprised at what he found: blocks of plastic explosive, detonators, webbing harness with pouches. Bolan was looking at a bomb factory. The Disciples of Khalfi had been preparing explosive devices to be worn by human carriers. It was the ultimate delivery system. Members of the sect would be able to walk the streets in comparative anonymity, placing themselves exactly where they wanted to be before setting off the explosive they were carrying. The plastique was an extremely powerful compound, and the amount being transported would detonate over a wide area, causing terrible damage to life and property. The fact that the Disciples were willing to sacrifice their own lives to their cause highlighted the depths of their dedication.

It was, as Harry Jordan had said, the kind of devotion that was near impossible to reason with.

A thorough search of the basement unearthed little solid information. A check of the bodies revealed less. None of the dead terrorists carried anything of use to Bolan. Other than what might be expected in any man's pockets, there was nothing of value.

Bolan located a telephone and punched in the number that would be rerouted and bounced off satellite dishes before it connected with an operator at Stony Man Farm. Even so, it took no longer than any normal telephone link. In seconds he was talking to Hal Brognola.

"You make contact?" the big Fed asked without preamble.

"Yeah."

"So?"

"We have a cozy little setup here in the Windy City," Bolan said. "Bomb factory in the basement, courtesy of the Disciples."

"Have you closed it down?"

"Maybe. Just before I went in a panel truck made a delivery. It also left with a package on board. I need two things—someone to take care of this hardware and a make on the license plate on that truck."

He repeated the number for Brognola.

"No problem. Striker, you get out of there. I don't want you around when the law arrives. I'll get the Bear to run that number through the system. Call in when you locate yourself."

"Will do."

"So get the hell out of there, and make it fast!"

6

Rain was still falling from a slate-gray dawn sky. Mack Bolan sat watching it bounce off the roof of a car parked outside the window of the diner. He pushed aside his empty breakfast plate and reached for the mug of strong black coffee.

He could hear the bland tones of a TV newscaster coming from the set on a shelf at the end of the counter. He had listened to the entire news program while he had been eating, and there had been no report that a bomb factory had been found within the city. Brognola had been successful in keeping the news away from the media.

Turning back to the window, Bolan saw a car turn into the diner's front lot and brake. The familiar lean figure of Jack Grimaldi climbed out, and he made his way inside the diner. The Stony Man flier ordered coffee as he passed the counter, then slid into the booth. He dragged off the long-peaked cap he was wearing and grinned across at Bolan.

"Long night?" he asked.

Bolan drained the rest of his coffee and waited until the waitress arrived with Grimaldi's mug and a steaming pot. She filled both mugs, gave the warrior a very friendly smile and returned to the counter.

"Looks obliging," Grimaldi remarked, eyeing her long legs.

"Too young for you, Jack."

"They're never too *young*," Grimaldi commented.

"Everything ready?" Bolan asked.

"Yeah. The chopper is juiced up and rarin' to go. Where to this time?"

"Colorado."

"You sure this is a genuine mission, Sarge? More like the daddy of all grand tours to me."

"Nobody promised it was going to be all fun, Jack."

"You can say that again. So who's in Colorado?"

"The name that keeps showing up every time we dig is Nori Hassad. Looks like he's the sleeper for this group. He's a successful businessman on the surface, but has his hand in all kinds of things. And he's got the financial clout to make things happen without too many questions being asked. Aaron has linked him with the Disciples, plus he has an interest in the Lebanese restaurant. We have the telephone connection with the terrorists back in Connecticut. The same number was on one of the guys I tangled with in New York. And now the panel truck I saw at the restaurant last night. It was a genuine registration. They probably thought it would be less likely to attract the attention of someone who ran a check and found stolen or phony plates. The truck belongs to a freighting company that operates out of Boulder, Colorado. Aaron had to do some hard digging, but he found that the freight outfit is a subsidiary of one of Hassad's larger companies."

"We heading for Boulder?"

Bolan drained his coffee, stood up, pulled out some money and dropped several bills on the table.

"Yes," he said. "Then Aspen."

"Aspen? What's there?"

"Nori Hassad's ski lodge, closed for renovations before the winter season starts."

Grimaldi followed him out of the diner.

"We shouldn't have problems getting reservations, then."

THE HELICOPTER DROPPED through the shimmering Colorado sky, coming in for a landing.

"You want me along?" Grimaldi asked as he shut down the aircraft's power.

"Thanks, but no, Jack. I need you as backup."

Bolan stepped out of the temperature-controlled interior of the combat chopper and felt the Colorado day close around him. It was hot. He took the zippered bag Grimaldi handed to him and turned as a jeep sped across the tarmac of the Air National Guard base at Buckley. Brognola had gained permission from the ANG for Bolan to land and for Grimaldi to stay there in case he was needed. As far as the ANG was concerned, the warrior was on government work and was to be given all the cooperation he needed. Bolan had already called in his requirements on the flight to Colorado.

The jeep rolled to a stop and a lean, tanned Guard lieutenant climbed out.

"Mr. Blanski, I'm Lieutenant Neeson."

Bolan nodded and put out his hand.

"I'm grateful for your help, Lieutenant, and I promise to be out of your hair fast."

The young officer smiled. "No need for that, sir. Only too glad we could help."

Grimaldi had stepped out of the helicopter and closed the hatch that prevented anyone but him from gaining access to the aircraft.

"That's some bird," Neeson said admiringly.

"She sure is," Grimaldi replied.

"I'll take you across to the main building. There's an office you can use, and it has a telephone with a direct line." Neeson handed the Executioner a card with the number typed on it.

Bolan and Grimaldi climbed into the rear of the Jeep. Neeson got behind the wheel and spun the vehicle in a tight circle.

"There's a rental waiting for you, Mr. Blanski, tanked up and ready to go. It's been fitted with a mobile phone."

The warrior tapped him on the shoulder. "Thanks for that."

The rental was a dark-colored Ford. Bolan dropped his bag on the front seat and turned to Grimaldi, waiting until Neeson had moved out of earshot.

"Hold the fort, Jack. I'll check in with you on a regular basis. If I need you in a hurry, I'll yell. Keep in touch with Stony Man in case anything breaks at their end."

"Will do. You watch your back, Sarge."

Bolan slipped behind the wheel and started the car. He raised a hand to Neeson as he took the Ford toward the main gate and out onto the highway.

According to the lieutenant, Boulder was just over an hour's drive away. If everything went according to plan, he would be there by midafternoon.

The warrior turned on the radio, picking up a station that was playing middle-of-the-road music. He turned it low, so that the music provided peaceful relief from the long drive.

He was trying to work out what the Disciples of Khalfi were planning. That they were after the members of the news team went without question. They had gone directly for the two people who had separated from the others. Eliminate them first, then go after the remaining three members of the group. As far as Bolan knew, the survivors still operated together as a team. He hoped Brognola would be able to pinpoint their whereabouts. The sooner he knew, the better he would like it. The terrorists had scored against Ras Fallil, but failed against Harry Jordan because Bolan had reached him in time.

It might not work out so neatly next time.

Bolan was still piecing things together, handling problems as they came along. He was working on instinct and information that was reaching him in fragments.

The bomb factory in Chicago was still fresh in his thoughts. It was out of commission now, but how many explosive devices had been shipped out before Bolan closed it down? Where had they gone—to the Disciples of Khalfi? To Islamic-fundamentalist sleepers who had been living and working in the U.S., men and women dedicated to the cause who were just waiting for the call to arms? How many of them were in the country? A dozen? Two dozen? A hundred? There could be an army of them, carrying out mundane tasks each day alongside unsuspecting Americans, working in a dozen cities across the country, smiling and polite as they went through each day, while behind the masks they were living for the call that would tell them the time had come for the supreme sacrifice. Whatever political-religious rhetoric might be used, it would be the task of the chosen man or woman to go out and enact their moment.

It was a chilling thought to Mack Bolan that because of America's willingness to accept the peoples of a troubled world, unwittingly she might be opening her doors to some who were not her friends, people who used the open door to gain access to a nation without borders or controls, to a vast continent that allowed its citizens free access. They could use that freedom, that welcome, to walk unhindered while they planned misdeeds that would bring pain and suffering to the people of America.

Bolan found he was gripping the steering wheel tightly, his knuckles showing white. Once before, he had stated that the real war was being fought at home in America, against an implacable enemy within its own borders. He had done much to decimate that enemy during his battle against the Mafia, and as much again during his terrorist wars. He was still waging that war. Sometimes it took him beyond the shores of America, and the objectives had been somewhat redefined. But when it came right down to it, Bolan was aware that there was still a need for someone to stand against the enemies of America at home. The nation still had its own troubles, problems that needed addressing. And if the enemies of the United States brought the war into the country itself, then they were going to have to wage it through Mack Bolan. There was too much at stake to allow the terrorists and fanatics to bring their grievances in-country.

Try they might, but they were going to have to be prepared to pay one hell of a price for that privilege.

And all of it in blood.

BOLAN MADE HIS FIRST check-in call as he approached Boulder.

"Jack, anything I need to know?"

"Stony Man called a short while ago. The panel truck you ID'd in Chicago was involved in a chase with the local cops near Boulder. Apparently there was a routine roadblock. The police were on the lookout for a hit-and-run driver. The driver of the panel truck must have panicked. Maybe he thought the roadblock was for the truck. He did a U-turn and took off. The cops went after him, and a few miles down the road the truck went off the road. The driver was killed, but his passenger was only injured. They took him to a local hospital."

"They find anything in the truck?"

"Yeah. A number of homemade explosive devices fixed to webbing harness like the ones you found in Chicago."

"Where is the guy now?"

"He's still in the hospital. Hal's got the cops standing guard over him until a special agent arrives. He wants the lid kept on this. The locals don't like it, but Hal's played the Fed to the hilt."

"I'm on my way," Bolan said, memorizing the information Grimaldi fed him about who was in charge and where the hospital was located.

He hoped the man in the hospital would respond to being questioned.

THE WARRIOR PULLED into the hospital parking lot around three o'clock in the afternoon. He parked the Ford, climbed out, locked the car and turned toward the three-story white building.

He noticed the two police cruisers near the main entrance, but other than that there was no unusual activity taking place in the area—which unsettled Bolan for some reason. He couldn't put a finger on it, but the scene felt unreal.

His eyes scanned the immediate area, taking in the cars parked in neat rows, the visitors moving back and forth between parking lot and hospital building. To his far left he could see the emergency entrance where the ambulances parked.

Everything looked peaceful, orderly, nothing out of place.

As the warrior stepped out from between the rows of parked cars and into the access lane, he picked up the low throb of an idling engine. It was behind him. He glanced over his shoulder as the sound rose in volume, and stared through the windshield of a light gray panel truck. Unmarked and anonymous, it was rolling slowly along the lane.

Bolan stepped aside as the truck reached him. It passed by, and the Executioner turned as the driver's door drew level with him.

The man behind the wheel stared straight ahead, his face taut, glistening with a faint sheen of perspiration. Beside him his passenger also gazed through the windshield with singular attention.

The truck pulled ahead of Bolan, still rolling slowly, and he caught a shadowy flicker of movement through the rear windows.

At that precise moment the vehicle accelerated with a roar, tires squealing as they burned against the pavement. The truck picked up speed as it rushed along the lane, heading directly for the hospital entrance.

Bolan pulled the Beretta and broke into a run.

The truck reached the end of the lane and made a sliding turn before coming to a lurching halt inches from one of the parked police cruisers. Doors burst open and a tight group of armed figures sprang from the rear of the vehicle. They broke apart, weapons up and tracking as they were confronted by the officers from the parked cruisers.

The peace and quiet of the hospital area was shattered by the harsh chatter of automatic gunfire. Bullets punched holes in metal, disintegrated glass and ravaged human flesh.

Two uniformed cops were down. One lay on his stomach, face to the pavement, dark streams of blood spreading out from his battered skull. His partner was crumpled against the cruiser's rear fender, attempting to stem the blood pulsing from his punctured side.

"Somebody help these men," Bolan shouted, drawing a young, wide-eyed doctor to the scene. The Executioner's firm tone catalyzed the man into action.

The policemen from the other cruiser raced across the lot, brandishing riot shotguns. They sighted Bolan and drew down on him.

."Hold it right there!" one yelled, taking in the scene. He spotted Bolan's drawn gun. "Son of a bitch, you get rid of that right now!"

"Easy, friend," the warrior said, holding out the ID badge he had just pulled from his pocket. "The perpetrators are inside."

The cop eyed the badge, then turned his steely gaze back on Bolan. "Yeah? So how'd you get here so damn fast?"

"I was on my way to interview the guy you people picked out of that wrecked panel truck. You were holding him for me."

"Right enough, Al," the second cop said. "Somebody said a fed was coming in."

Bolan nodded. "That's me. Now let's move before that guy's friends kill anyone else."

"Heck, we got two of our buddies guarding that mother!"

"You two take the emergency entrance," Bolan suggested. "Come in from the other side. I'll go in this way."

"Prisoner's on the second floor, west wing, room 203."

"You guys watch yourselves with these people," Bolan warned. "Don't cut them any slack."

Pushing to his feet, the warrior headed for the main entrance.

The entrance lobby was in total confusion. The Executioner picked his way through the dazed people, noticing that a number of bodies were on the floor. The sight angered him, the images of ordinary citizens sprawled in loose postures, blood glistening wetly on flesh and clothing, splashed across the smooth, polished floor.

He hit the stairs at a dead run, taking them three at a time, his eyes and his gun on the prowl, searching the way ahead, seeking the enemy.

The Disciples of Khalfi had shown themselves, coming out into the open and defying the laws, denying the respect due to the country they had covertly entered.

Their actions had lost them any consideration they might have been allowed. As far as Mack Bolan was concerned, these terrorists had defiled the streets of America too long already. This time they had taken that one step too many.

As he reached the second-floor landing and turned in the direction of the corridor that would take him to room 203, Bolan heard a commotion. It was followed by the ugly chatter of an autoweapon, and screams. Glass shattered and objects crashed to the floor as people scattered from the bullets spraying from the terrorists' weapons.

Turning the corner, Bolan was faced by a scene of bloody chaos. A number of bodies were sprawled on the floor, some moving, others still. Blood soaked through clothing, pooled on the floor or ran down the pristine walls.

At the far end of the corridor the three terrorists were spread in a loose bunch, trading shots with two uniformed police officers. The cops were backed into a corner, aware of their vulnerability, but still defying the invaders.

One policeman triggered his weapon and fired two well-placed slugs in the upper chest of one terrorist, knocking him back against the wall. Before he could follow up, the cop was stitched from chest to groin by a sustained burst from one of the Disciples. He went down without a sound, the front of his body erupting bloody gouts.

The surviving policeman grasped his weapon two-fisted and swung it around to fire, stepping in front of his downed partner to protect him.

That was when Bolan dealt himself into the game, dropping the closer terrorist with a 3-round burst through the back of the gunner's skull. The 9 mm tumblers exploded from his startled face in a bloody geyser, and the terrorist was pitched forward, uttering a single, stunned grunt before crashing facedown on the polished floor.

Swiveling the Beretta in a tight arc, the warrior terminated the wounded terrorist as he struggled to rejoin the battle, lifting his autoweapon in a gesture of defiance. The slugs caught him in the chest, cleaving his heart. He slithered crablike along the wall, trailing a smear of red before he pitched to the floor.

Advancing along the corridor, Bolan snapped off a burst at the surviving terrorist, missing the man by a fraction as he dodged in through the door of room 203, slamming it shut behind him.

Bolan hit the door flat out, flinging it back against the inner wall. As he entered the room he heard the harsh crackle of autofire and took a dive across the floor, then realized the shots hadn't been directed at him. He came up on one knee, the Beretta tracking across the room.

The terrorist stood at the foot of the room's single bed, his weapon directed at the writhing figure under the bloody covers. The wounded terrorist from the wrecked panel truck, bandaged and wired up to monitors, gasped his final agonized breaths in those brief seconds. His body had been torn apart by the close-range blast from his brother Disciple's weapon.

Bolan's finger caressed the 93-R's trigger as the surviving terrorist twisted away from the bed, a wild yell of defiance erupting from his lips as he brought around his weapon. The 3-round burst hit him in the head, spinning him off balance and tumbling him across the room. He fell in a writhing heap against the wall, the subgun spilling from his nerveless fingers.

"God Almighty, what the hell was all that about?"

Bolan glanced around.

The surviving cop was standing in the open doorway, his face pale from shock, his gun hanging limply at his side. He rubbed absently at the blood on his cheek—blood from his wounded partner.

"They came for their partner," Bolan answered, indicating the dead terrorist on the bed. "They either took him out alive, or made sure he couldn't talk."

Outside in the corridor members of the medical staff were shrugging off their own feelings and attending to the wounded. Security alarms were ringing, drowning the cries of the patients frightened by the violent interruption to the normal, orderly pattern of life in the hospital.

"Hey, buddy, who are you anyhow?" the cop asked as the warrior walked by him.

Bolan showed his ID.

"I came to talk to him," he explained to the policeman, indicating the man on the bed.

"Who are these damn people? I mean, where do they think they are? This isn't Beirut."

A grim smile edged Bolan's mouth. Not yet, he thought, but if they had their way...

The thought chilled him, and he determined that it would never happen in America as long as he was able to do anything about it.

7

Nori Hassad approached the room with an unease that made his stomach churn. Beyond the closed door Rachim Gazli was giving full rein to his rage and fury. His deep, powerful voice penetrated the heavy closed door and seemed directed at Hassad himself.

Pausing at the threshold, his hand hesitating close to the doorknob, Hassad listened to Gazli's harangue. The leader of the strike team was berating his assembled brothers as if the death of their companions was their fault alone. Hassad debated whether he should go away and return when the man had calmed down. That was if Gazli *did* calm down. His rage seemed to be getting out of control. It was a side to his character that Hassad hadn't experienced up to this point, and it frightened him.

Though he was responsible for arranging the needs of the strike team as they prepared for their mission in America, and even though he knew and accepted that they would use extreme violence against their targets, Hassad wasn't a man of violence himself. He was in total agreement as to what needed to be done in the name of Khalfi, but he didn't want to be witness to the actual deed. Physical brutality repulsed him. The sight of blood and injury made him ill. He couldn't bear to watch American television with its preoccupation with violence both as entertainment and news.

Hassad was a true believer. His faith in the Islamic vision was unshakable, but he used his faith to help others, as he was doing for Gazli. There was a need for the terrorist's way—this he truly believed. And Hassad could turn away from the terrible things done in the name of Khalfi, because they were just and needful. The Americans understood violence. It was part of the national makeup, something they were born to accept and to employ when all else failed. America was fueled by violence in many forms. It was as much an American thing as apple pie and saluting the flag. It reached far back into American history. The nation had been forged through violence, first against the American Indians and then American against American. It flowed through folklore and became entrenched within the American psyche. It was the only way to make the country sit up and take notice.

The Americans had betrayed Ayatollah Khalfi and had been instrumental in his death.

Death by violence.

So they would be paid in kind, made to see that their precious land wasn't invulnerable, that a small band of dedicated believers, united through their devotion to Khalfi, could destroy the ones responsible in their own country. All the world would see that America was as weak as other nations when it came to resisting the wrath of Islam.

That said, Hassad still found he was reluctant to enter the room and witness Gazli's verbal violence. The thunderous litany, penetrating the thick door, made him cringe. His heart pounded, and beads of sweat popped out across his forehead. His trembling became too much for him to bear, and he turned and hurried away, back through the sprawling lodge to the sanctuary of his spacious office.

Closing the door, Hassad crossed to stand in front of the huge picture window that looked out across the snowcapped mountain peaks. Above them the blue and cloudless sky filled the horizon. Closer to the lodge the undulating landscape soothed him. He felt his trembling cease after a while. Breathing deeply, Hassad leaned his heated face against the cool glass of the window.

The natural beauty of the Colorado high country drew him as it always did. There was something about this majestic country he felt part of. When he viewed it he felt sad that it was wasted on the Americans, a nation of greedy opportunists, too busy slaughtering one another to realize the majesty of their land. Down in the grubby, dark cities, they fought over property and possessions, killed one another for money, drugs and sex and forgot the stunning wonders of their nation. It took a stranger to see.

Nori Hassad had come to America, accepted its ways to pursue his own. He had profited, using the gullibility of the Americans to make his fortune. They were so naive in many ways, easily duped and ready to come back for more. He manipulated and traded, making shrewd investments, plowing his money and expertise back into his ventures. His fortune grew. His standing in the business community expanded until he was an accepted member. And all the time he was quietly making his plans, building his organization with the help of loyal, true members of the Islamic faith, men and women who were ready to sacrifice themselves come the day of reckoning.

And the call did come—from the Disciples of Khalfi.

At first everything seemed to be going well. Gazli and his people had arrived, spread out between Colorado and New York. Once established, they had started to search out their targets, the news team responsible for the death of Ayatollah Khalfi.

First was the traitor Ras Fallil. He had been located in New York and dealt with.

At the same time the sister of the American named Harry Jordan had been taken captive and made to talk, to reveal the whereabouts of her vanished brother.

But then things had started to go wrong.

The Disciples searching Fallil's apartment in New York had been surprised by an American—policeman or agent, no one knew. One of the Disciples died instantly. The other escaped, wounded, but managed to inform Gazli before killing himself to avoid being arrested.

Soon after that the safehouse in Connecticut had been breached. Again brothers had died, and Jordan's sister was removed to safety.

Worse still, the restaurant in Chicago had been subject to attack. All inside had died, and the bomb-making facility was now in the hands of the American authorities.

Even the attack on the hospital had been terminated, though the wounded brother had been sacrificed to prevent his talking. The local TV station had broadcast a brief item about the vehicle accident, showing the damaged panel truck, which had been identified by its license plate.

It was, Hassad admitted, a catalog of setbacks. It had compromised their security, made the operation more difficult. None of them had even considered terminating the mission. That could not—would not—happen.

Gazli would see the mission through even if he was the last brother alive. On his hands and knees, with his lifeblood draining away, he would crawl through fire to complete it.

No one would be allowed to jeopardize the sacred mission. It *had* to succeed. The *fatwa* had been declared, and it couldn't be withdrawn. It was forbidden to even raise such thoughts.

The strain was beginning to affect Hassad. Though he had longed to be a part of some important event so that he could actively support his more militant brethren, he was finding that living on the edge was hard. Perhaps he had spent too much time in America sampling the good life and forgetting his real purpose. Deeply immersed in business and the allure of money-making, Hassad's resolve had been weakened to a degree. His spiritual desire to help wasn't matched by his physical ability to cope with the pressures.

Hassad turned to his desk and opened a drawer. He took out a box of fine cigars, selected one and clipped off the end with a gold-plated cutter presented to him by a grateful business associate. He lit the cigar with a wooden match from a box he kept in the drawer and drew in the rich, aromatic smoke. The aroma soothed him. He sank into his leather executive chair, leaning back and swiveling so he could take in the scene beyond the window again, reviewing the situation as he enjoyed the cigar.

Gazli had made it clear that he still wanted the explosive devices, which meant Hassad would need to make contact with his supplier once again. The original purchase had cost a great deal, but the money meant nothing. It was the need to make contact with the supplier. He was an American who had little regard for anything but making money and trading in his illegal weapons and explosives. He was based in Santa Fe and ran a lucrative business, supplying arms to anyone who had the cash. His contacts were spread far and wide across the country and overseas. Rumor had it that he could supply anything, from the smallest handgun all the way up to a battle tank. Hassad could well believe it. He didn't like the man, but he had learned early in his dealings with the Americans that it didn't matter that you disliked a business associate, just as long as you got what you wanted out of the deal.

Facing his desk again, Hassad reached for the telephone and punched in a number that connected him with a toneless voice on a recorder. He left his message and replaced the receiver. Twenty minutes later, just as he finished his cigar, the phone rang. Hassad picked it up and recognized the thin, nasal voice of the dealer.

"I need a repeat order," Hassad said. "Exactly the same as last time. Arrangements as before. But I require the order to be filled urgently. Can you oblige?"

"Of course."

"Will the terms be the same?"

"As a gesture of goodwill against future dealings, I won't charge you extra. Give me two hours and I'll confirm."

Hassad put down the receiver. So far, so good.

The door opened and Gazli came into the office. He closed the door and crossed to stand by the desk, watching Hassad.

"I have just negotiated for more explosives. My contact will be calling back in a couple of hours to confirm."

Gazli didn't respond. His gaze was unflinching and Hassad could tell by the hard set of his mouth that the man was still angry.

"Rachim, we must be cautious. The Americans are not all the mindless fools we sometimes take them to be. Too many things have fallen by the wayside not to be noticed. Someone, somewhere, may be fitting separate incidents together and finding a pattern."

Gazli took a sharp intake of air.

"Are you telling me I should retreat? Pack my bags and go back home?" The last sentence was delivered with a trace of a smile. "If you knew me you wouldn't even think such a thing."

"I was not suggesting anything like that. Rachim, I want you to succeed. We all want that. But we have to consider the options. By all means go ahead. Why do you think I have arranged new supplies of explosives for you? My advice is intended to protect you. Do not underestimate the Americans. Believe me when I say I know them well. Remember I have lived here for a long time."

"Perhaps too long."

"You go too far, Rachim," Hassad snapped, leaning forward. "No one questions my loyalty."

"I am not questioning your loyalty, Nori Hassad. I was simply wondering just who you are loyal to. Islam, or your American bank account?"

8

Bolan drove by the entrance to the freight-company yard and parked the car beside a closed, deserted diner. He adjusted the rearview mirror so he could observe the gates from where he sat.

The chill of the Colorado night enveloped the car. A soft wind coming in over the flats outside town pushed fine dust across the deserted highway, leaving a fine mist over the windshield.

Easing off his leather jacket, Bolan adjusted the Beretta's shoulder holster. He wore his blacksuit, its slit pockets containing a selection of weapons for silent kills, while his handguns would take care of any opposition with less than silent techniques. Unzipping the bag on the seat beside him he took out the belt and holster that held the big Desert Eagle and strapped it around his waist. Taking out the powerful handgun, the warrior checked that it was fully loaded and ready for action. He had spare magazines for the big .44 and the Beretta stowed in pouches on his belt.

Bolan checked his watch. It was coming up to nine o'clock. During his time parked adjacent to the yard, only one vehicle had entered. Beyond the high perimeter fence, security lamps threw stark pools of light across the inner compound. There were only a few people about. A man was seated inside the small wooden hut that served as security, and on the far side of the compound Bolan could see lights blazing within the service bays as night crews worked on vehicles.

He was about to exit the car when he spotted lights approaching along the highway. The Executioner settled back and watched.

A light-colored limousine rolled up to the gates. The driver stepped out and spoke to the security man, who raised an arm and activated the barrier. The limo glided inside and coasted across the compound. Bolan watched its progress and saw it draw to a stop at a building in the far corner of the compound. At first glance the building appeared deserted, but after a few moments a rollup door opened and the limo eased inside. The door was then lowered.

Bolan's curiosity was aroused by the maneuver. He climbed out of the car, locked it and slipped the key safely away in one of his blacksuit pockets. Crossing the road well beyond the reach of the compound's lights, the night warrior circled the perimeter until he was able to approach it close to the building the limo entered. Crouched in the darkness, Bolan studied the fence. It was close to ten feet high, of chain-link construction, with thick concrete posts supporting the mesh. There were no signs of any alarms or detectors, and the fence certainly wasn't electrified. Bolan spent a good ten minutes checking the barrier carefully, in case he'd missed anything. Finally satisfied, he selected one of the concrete posts at the farthest corner and used it to scale the fence.

Once committed, Bolan went up and over without pause. He shinnied down the inner side, dropping the final six feet and landing without a sound. On his knees in the dust, the warrior took stock of his immediate surroundings.

He picked up the distant noise coming from the service bays. Focusing in closer, he listened for anything that might suggest a patrolling guard.

His caution was rewarded by the soft footfalls of someone walking in his direction.

Bolan moved quickly across to the wall of the building, pressed tight against the rough surface, and removed a garrote from a pocket in his blacksuit. Gripping the wooden handles at each end, he held himself motionless, waiting for the approaching man to show himself.

The sentry was clad in lightweight dark clothing. Even in the dim light Bolan was able to make out his dark features and black hair. The man carried a suppressed Ingram M-10, and a compact transceiver clipped to his belt, next to a holstered autopistol.

Bolan formed a loop with the garrote wire, his fists crossed as he waited for the guard to step by.

The Disciple of Khalfi, his eyes wandering to search the empty sky overhead, failed to hear the whisper of Death as it detached itself from the wall behind him. Nothing warned him what was about to happen, his first indication the cold snap of the thin wire as it dug into his flesh.

The dark sky seemed to blossom with hazy stars. As his body was denied air, the guard began to panic. He dropped his weapon and tried to claw at the offending wire, but it was already embedded in his flesh. Blood began to ooze around the wire from his sliced skin, making his fingers slick. Soft bubbling sounds forced themselves past his lips. The soft night became cold and hostile. The guard struggled wildly, only hastening his demise.

The Executioner increased the pressure on the garrote. He slammed a knee into the guy's spine, pulling him back so his shuddering body curved like a bow. With a final spasm the terrorist became still. Bolan lowered the corpse to the ground, dragging it out of sight close to the base of the wall. Pocketing the garrote, the warrior quickly retrieved the guard's dropped Ingram. He checked that the weapon was ready for use, then turned and made a circuit of the dark building, searching for other guards.

He almost ran headlong into the guy. The guard was moving fast, Ingram in one hand, his transceiver in the other, and Bolan realized he had probably been attempting to contact his partner.

Finesse was not the order of the day this time. Bolan swung the captured Ingram in a brutal arc, slamming the heavy suppressor under the man's chin. It snapped the terrorist's head back, with a dark stream of blood issuing from his mouth where he'd bitten into his tongue. As the guy staggered from the blow, Bolan closed in, delivering a powerful snap kick that connected with the guard's ribs. The man fell backward, his shoulders thudding against the building wall. He made a last-ditch effort to bring his Ingram into action but the warrior's own weapon, still being used as a club, slammed down across his wrist. Bone snapped and the MAC-10 tumbled to the ground. Bolan reversed the sweep of the Ingram, hammering it against the guy's skull. He delivered a trio of heavy blows, driving the guard to the ground. Ascertaining that the man was out of the action, the warrior moved on.

He found a small outbuilding attached to the side of the main building. It was the kind of structure that would house a compressor to supply air to equipment within the workshop. Above it Bolan spotted a window. Light showed through the dirty glass. He used an empty fuel drum to gain access to the outbuilding roof, and, leaning against the main wall, he was able to peer through the window.

The limo stood in a pool of light, flanked by a dusty 4×4. Nearby was a long workbench, surrounded by a group of six men who watched as a seventh, seated on a stool, worked on some apparatus. As far away as he was, Bolan was able to see the blocks of plastique and the body harness. They were identical to the ones he had seen in the bomb factory in Chicago.

The Executioner checked out the figures around the workbench. Two of them were Caucasian, the rest darker skinned. The area was littered with automatic weapons.

It seemed to Bolan that he had his evidence.

About to move away from the window, he spotted a figure walking toward the group, talking excitedly. He waved a transceiver at them and gesticulating wildly. Bolan couldn't hear what he was saying, but he didn't need to. He knew exactly what was going on.

He pulled back from the window, turned to climb back down from the outbuilding roof and found himself face-to-face with a man who brandished an Ingram subgun.

Bolan had picked up the moving figure even as he was completing his turn. The barrel of the Ingram had almost completed its upswing when the warrior locked eyes with the gunner.

He realized the man was in the process of easing back on the trigger, and dropped flat on the roof within the space of a heartbeat. The suppressed 9 mm slugs hissed over his prone form, shattering the window.

Before the gunman could alter his aim and pick up his stretched-out form, Bolan let himself slide closer to the edge, his own weapon probing the air before him. As he reached the roofline, the warrior triggered the MAC-10, sending a long burst into the motionless figure below him. The stream of slugs hammered through the guy's skull, penetrating the brain and into the torso, angling off in all directions. The fatally hit gunman stumbled backward, his body oozing blood from a half-dozen exit wounds.

Gripping the edge of the roof, the Executioner picked up the sound of distant yelling as other armed men began to converge on the outbuilding. He knew he didn't have long to decide on his next move.

The warrior judged the distance to the ground and the need to cover a number of yards of exposed ground before he could find cover away from the main building.

Easing back from the edge of the roof, Bolan backtracked, up the angled slope to the window, now practically free of glass. A quick glance inside confirmed what he had expected—the group gathered around the workbench had disappeared, probably to join in the hunt for the intruder, and they had left the man at the bench alone except for a single armed guard.

Bolan got a grip on the inside frame of the window and eased himself through the gap. He placed one foot on the twelve-inch ledge, then drew the rest of his body through. For a scant second he remained there, peering down into the building and weighing his options. They gave no guarantees either way. He tucked the Ingram close to his chest, let go of the windowframe and jumped.

The concrete floor rushed up to meet him. Bolan landed and rolled, feeling the impact jolt his legs. His forward motion took him in a powered roll, over his left shoulder and across the floor. He pushed the pain to the back of his mind, bracing himself as he skidded over the concrete, then got to his feet and brought the Ingram into play as he saw the armed guard turn to face him.

Bolan's MAC-10 exhaled its burst of 9 mm death, catching the guard chest high and flinging him back across the workbench. The guy on the stool scrambled to one side, half falling off his seat, snatching up the autopistol he had stashed nearby. The Executioner's second burst caught him in the left shoulder, tearing a bloody hole in the soft flesh. The man fell across the bench, still managing to get a grip on the pistol. He half turned in Bolan's direction before the warrior emptied his weapon's magazine into him, shredding his upper chest and throat. He spilled off the edge of the bench and crashed facedown on the concrete.

Moving to the workbench, Bolan quickly scanned the explosives laid out across its surface. His experienced eye recognized detonators and timing devices. The blocks of explosive had been fashioned into shapes that would fit the pouches attached to the harness constructions. He knew what they were intended for—human bombs.

The armed devices would be worn by volunteers who could wear them beneath street clothes and walk to a chosen place before detonating the explosives, a sacrifice for the carrier and a brutal death for the unknowing victims.

Bolan could hear the numbers falling inside his head. Time was running out. He examined the devices, which were complete except for the final connections to the timers. Bolan completed the connections and touched the keys on the compact timers, setting them to detonate in one minute, then activated the devices. The small readout dials flickered, the seconds beginning their descent to zero.

Bolan turned on his heel and ran across the floor to where the limo was parked. He leaned inside and saw that the key was in the ignition. He slid onto the seat and pulled the door shut, unlimbering the Desert Eagle and laying it on the seat beside him. Turning the key, he fired up the powerful engine. Locking the safety belt, he jammed his foot down on the gas and the heavy vehicle surged forward, tires squealing on the concrete, raising a cloud of smoke as they fought for traction.

A small door set in the wall beside the roller doors burst open, and figures armed with subguns raced into the building. The air was suddenly alive with streams of slugs as they concentrated their fire on the limo as it picked up speed. Bolan felt the impact of the gunfire, then realized the bullets were having little effect. A grim smile edged his lips as he offered silent thanks to whoever had decided a bullet-proof vehicle was needed.

Blurred figures pulled themselves away from the hurtling limo as Bolan pushed the pedal to the floor. One man didn't move fast enough, and the warrior felt the solid thud as the gunner was hit by the car. There was a strangled cry as the guy was bounced over the hood and into the windshield. The impact left a red smear on the glass after his broken form was catapulted over the vehicle's roof.

The roller door filled Bolan's field of vision. He gripped the steering wheel and braced himself for impact. There was a slight hesitation in the car's forward movement as it struck the door, then the thin aluminum tore apart with surprising ease and Bolan was out of the building, hauling the wheel back in line as he sped across the outer compound. He took the vehicle in the direction of the exit and hit the wooden barrier doing seventy. Yanking the wheel around, he pushed the limo along the highway, and when he reached the diner he swerved in behind it. Snatching the Desert Eagle from the seat, Bolan sprinted to his rental car, fished out his key, unlocked the door and slid behind the wheel.

As he turned the key to start the engine, he heard the roar of the first device he had set to detonate. He saw the bright glare of the second detonation moments later, followed by the rumble of the explosion. Hauling the wheel around, Bolan gunned the engine and headed toward the highway.

As he eased by the abandoned limo, the 4 × 4 that had been parked inside the workshop sped by. The driver stamped on the brake as the limo was spotted, sending the 4×4 into a bouncing halt. Engine howling, the off-road vehicle began to reverse.

Bolan pushed his foot down hard and took the rental car along the highway, passing the freight yard just ahead of two more vehicles as they nosed onto the road. Glancing in his rearview mirror, he saw the pair of vehicles fall in behind the 4×4 as it took up the pursuit.

The Executioner settled back in his seat, pushing his vehicle to the limit as he attempted to lose his deadly pursuers.

9

Thick clouds of white dust spumed up behind the rental as Mack Bolan held his foot to the floor. The car barreled into the darkness, headlights cleaving the gloom ahead.

To where?

The warrior posed the question in his mind, came up with no answer and dismissed the problem. He was going to have to wing this one, execute his moves as and when he made them.

A man of lesser qualities might have cursed and damned his bad luck, blamed everything and everyone for the way things had gone against him. Bolan simply accepted the turn of events and looked ahead, not backward. Whether it was down to ill luck or his own bad judgment, it made no difference. It wasn't the first time, less likely to be the last, that low-key penetrations, intended to gain information prior to decisive action, had turned around and presented him with sudden, violent resistance. It was the nature of warfare that carefully laid plans had a habit of biting the initiator. Perversity had no favorites. Bolan was fighting a just war by any standards, yet his personal battle against evil didn't protect him from the pitfalls of life. The warrior had come to terms with that bare fact a long time ago, as far back as Vietnam, when good friends died before his eyes, and he walked away from it all intact.

He had learned a hard lesson during his time in the Asian hellgrounds—that truth and decency were no magic cloaks to shield the good guys. They could, and did, suffer and die. Many returned home shattered hulks who never came to terms with the experience of war, sound in body, but with minds turned away from reality by the horrors they had experienced. Some took it and learned to live with the shadows. Others let it fester and rot their thinking. They turned bitter, frustrated, and let their lives slip away.

Bolan had known his share of tragedy in Vietnam and also back home. He lost out twice over. But there was something inside the man that refused to surrender. He never forgot what he'd lost, but instead of allowing it to eat away his soul, he decided to do something about it.

He did.

And he was still doing something.

This time it was one-to-one with terrorists who had imported their proclaimed war against America onto the continent itself. Crossing the border, they had cast the shadow of their fanatical crusade across the land. They hadn't reckoned on Mack Bolan pitching in to put a stop to their insidious plans, but they were beginning to become aware of his presence. The hard way.

Bolan drove hard and fast, leading his pursuers away from the urban area and into the rocky terrain where he could choose the time and place for a confrontation.

The Executioner wasn't running from a fight; he was leading his enemies to a battle.

Passing a weathered rock formation he had noted on his drive in earlier that afternoon, Bolan looked for the turn that led to a dirt road cutting off across country. He had filed away the details of the turnoff, logging it as a possible escape route if the need arose. He'd spotted the dirt road less than a quarter mile before the rock formation on his drive in. Now he recalled it in reverse, and as the car's headlights picked up the turnoff, Bolan spun the wheel and took the car into a rocking slide, kicking up thick clouds of dust.

The vehicle's wheels spun for a few seconds, then gained traction on the gravel surface of the unpaved road. Bolan held the wheel firmly, countering the drifting effect of the loose surface under the tires.

The undulating land, dotted with islands of upthrust rock and clumps of brush and trees, spread out before him. He pushed the vehicle as hard as he could, allowing that it wasn't primarily designed for off-road travel. Right now it was a means to an end, a lure meant to draw his pursuers.

Bolan checked his odometer. He had driven just over a mile from the highway.

Glancing in the rearview mirror, he spotted the bouncing headlight beams of the pursuing vehicles. They had lost some ground, having overshot the turn. Now they were pushing as hard as Bolan, and perhaps congratulating themselves over what they would consider the upcoming victory.

The Executioner drove between eroded arches of rock, turning the vehicle down a long slope that led to a wide, shallow basin. He decided that this was close to perfect for what he wanted.

Once he had made his decision, he acted on it without further thought. Picking up the Desert Eagle, Bolan reached across and unlatched his door. He took his foot off the gas pedal and allowed the speed to drop before rolling out of his seat and taking a long, low dive into the first clump of brush that loomed up out of the shadows. The brush broke the warrior's fall as he shoulder-rolled, then lay prone on the ground.

The rental bounced down the slope, staying on line for several yards before the wheel spun and the car executed a quarter circle before grinding to a halt.

The pursuing trio of vehicles, led by the ground-breaking 4 × 4, swept by Bolan's prone form, enveloping him in swirling dust.

The convoy braked to an untidy stop partway down the slope. Roaring engines were shut down. From his place of concealment Bolan could hear the sudden outburst of voices as each man tried to set into motion his own particular plan of action.

Cars doors slammed as the occupants made their exits. The metallic clicks of weapons being cocked sounded sharply in the night air.

Men conversed in Farsi, yet others in English with strident American accents.

Their intention, in any language, was clear—they were out to kill the man who had invaded their secretive and highly illegal meeting.

Mack Bolan had no intention of allowing them to achieve their objective.

He pushed to his feet, keeping low as he circled around the assembled group.

The warrior reached the rearmost car just as the wheelman decided to step out and watch what was happening. The driver stepped away from his open door, handgun dangling loosely at his side, stretching his neck to see how his partners were faring, which was as far as he got.

The 93-R rose out of the darkness, the muzzle settling briefly before Bolan stroked the trigger, sending a triburst into the back of the driver's skull. The man was catapulted forward against his open door, and he collapsed without a sound, curling in a tight heap against the bottom of the door.

Easing along the side of the car, Bolan peered in through the rear window of the vehicle ahead. The driver of this one hadn't bothered to step out. He was sitting behind his steering wheel, busy lighting a cigarette. His attention was everywhere but on the moment, which was his last.

The 3-round burst that Bolan drilled through the car's rear window shattered the glass, then punched ugly holes in the driver's skull, driving his head forward into the padded rim of the steering wheel.

The sudden blare of the car's horn, activated by the pressure of the dead man's head weighing down on the pad, was totally unexpected. The strident sound blasted through the comparative silence, jarring nerves and causing instant reactions.

The probing muzzles of hostile weapons were turned in Bolan's general direction, and a yell of recognition went up as one sharp-eyed gunman caught a fleeting impression of Mack Bolan's dark form moving between two of the parked cars.

A ragged volley of gunfire punctuated the warning, the wild fire striking vehicles, imploding windows.

Someone shouted for a cease-fire, but the warning came too late.

Bolan's Beretta, held two-fisted, tracked in on the shadow behind one of the muzzle-flashes. He triggered a triburst that caught the unsuspecting terrorist in the throat, tossing him backward. The gunman hit the ground, spasms twisting his body, a final gargling moan escaping from bloody lips.

The moment he had fired, Bolan crouched and moved, spacing himself from the immediate area. Pressed against a sand-scoured rock, he raised the Beretta again and watched for movement. He picked out the slow-moving shape of an armed man. Shoulders hunched, weapon held hip high, the gunner was casting around, hesitant, unsure of where he should be looking. He was also aware of being out in the open, vulnerable to any shot coming out of the darkness.

The cold muzzle of the 93-R settled on target, and Bolan stroked the trigger. His three 9 mm slugs punched in through flesh and muscle, tearing a bloody path to the hardman's heart. He pitched over sideways, his finger tightening against the trigger of his autoweapon. The ground around him erupted, dirt and stone fragments spraying the air. Then he hit facedown, his finger relaxing as he flopped over on his side.

Bolan was about to change his position when he sensed someone close. He turned to look over his shoulder and saw a dark figure bearing down on him. The gunner was running hard, his autoweapon held tight against his chest. He was seeking cover, and, by some decree of fate, had picked out the spot where the warrior was crouching.

The Executioner raised the Beretta and triggered his final 3-round burst, drilling the 9 mm slugs into the hardman's chest. He kept running for another half dozen steps before his body realized it was no longer receiving signals from the brain. He crashed face first into the ground, his body shuddering in reaction to the final surges in his nervous system.

Now Bolan moved, jamming the empty Beretta into its holster and replacing it with the massive .44 Magnum Desert Eagle.

He broke away from his covering rock and sprinted across an empty stretch of terrain. His destination was a scattering of boulders and brush roughly twenty feet away.

Bolan had almost reached the cover of the boulders when he picked up a shouted call behind him, which was followed by the angry crackle of autofire. Off-target slugs caromed off the rocks ahead of him, spinning into the darkness. Changing direction, the warrior veered to the left, away from the volley, drawing his pursuers.

He cleared a flat boulder, dropped to his knees behind it, then turned and rested the Desert Eagle across the rock, braced by his clenched fists. His eyes, well adjusted to the gloom, picked out the three most eager of his enemies. They were closing in fast, starting to spread, when the big sound of the .44 exploded out of the night.

Bolan fired three shots, close enough to roll out in perfect harmony, yet predetermined enough for him to isolate each target. The 240-grain hollowpoints achieved their purpose with body-stopping velocity. The racing terrorists were halted in their tracks, blood and debris spurting briefly as the express impact of the heavy slugs tore ragged holes in their flesh. Down and dying, they slid into a darkness that was deeper and longer than the night they had just exited.

An autoweapon opened up to Bolan's right. The gunner was close, his shots scoring the surface of the rock concealing the Executioner. Bolan pulled back, feeling stone chips raised by the slugs stinging his cheek. He dropped lower behind his boulder, knowing that the covering fire would have given vital time to anyone wanting to close in on his position.

The warrior stayed down, ears straining, and after a few seconds he heard the soft slaps of running feet. Someone was approaching from his left, cutting across the open ground.

The covering gunner delivered a second burst.

As the shots faded, Bolan eased around, gauging where the running man would make his appearance.

When he did show, autoweapon brandished in both hands, his wild-eyed yelling intended to throw his target off guard, he was no more than a few feet from where Bolan had anticipated.

The finality of the confrontation became dependent on whoever reacted faster.

Bolan's adversary was a terrorist capable of brutal atrocities carried out through deceit and treachery, and done at a distance. He lacked the cool efficiency required for a face-to-face showdown. It took a great deal of self-control and up-front courage to confront a hostile gun at close quarters.

The Disciple of Khalfi, though prepared to die for his cause, hadn't expected to give his life that night. Backed by his brothers, ranged against a single man, he had expected a swift victory. That had been suddenly reversed, leaving the terrorist exposed and unable to back down. So he went through the motions of combat, carrying a dread feeling deep inside that he was acting out of bravado rather than wisdom.

The black-clad American confronting him seemed to have no feelings of inadequacy.

Rising from a crouch, his arms extended, the shadow warrior thrust out his arms, both hands clamped around the butt of the huge handgun he carried.

The terrorist found himself staring into the black hole of the muzzle for what seemed an eternity. His own weapon felt frozen in his hands, and when he tried to line it up his movements were sluggish.

By some miracle his finger pulled back on the trigger, and he told himself that he was going to fire first, after all.

And then the world vanished in a brilliant glare of red that turned to stark white. The night turned silent and empty. Then there was nothing.

Mack Bolan was moving even before the terrorist hit the ground. There was at least one more out in the darkness—the man who had laid down the covering fire—and possibly others, hidden in the shadows.

The warrior moved swiftly in the general direction the gunfire had come from. As he neared the spot he heard distant footsteps, someone running—but away rather than toward him.

He held back, the Desert Eagle probing the shadows. Instinct warned him that to go on was to invite trouble. The retreating gunman seemed to be beckoning him, wanting Bolan to follow.

Then he heard the muted roar of a car engine starting up.

Bolan spun on his heel. He needed to vacate the area in case the escapee called in backup. His mission was finished here. The enemy had been decimated, and the warrior's campaign dictated that he move forward.

The rattle of hardware caught his ears, coming from two directions. One was slightly behind and to his left, the other on his right-hand side and ahead.

Powerful flashlights pierced the darkness, the forward one playing directly into his eyes. The hard muzzle of a weapon was jammed into Bolan's spine, the force of the jab indicating that the gunner was in earnest.

"Move and you die here!"

Which meant they wanted him alive for the time being. Bolan accepted the compromise. As a live captive, there was at least a chance. Once he was dead it all ended. He allowed the muzzle of the Desert Eagle to sag groundward. A moment later it was yanked from his fingers. A hand reached out and took the Beretta.

"You will come with us. Now."

To add emphasis to the spoken word, a hand materialized from the shadows and delivered a jarring slap to the side of Bolan's face. The backhanded blow was hard, a heavy ring on one finger gouging a bloody furrow across Bolan's jawline, drawing blood.

The shadowy figures pushed and jostled the warrior as they directed him to the 4 × 4.

Bolan was slammed against the side of the vehicle. The flashlights were held on his face, denying him the opportunity of seeing his captors. The combat harness was unbuckled and removed, and he was subjected to a thorough body search. The pockets of his blacksuit were emptied.

The shadow men exchanged subdued words. They spoke in Farsi, adding final confirmation of their identity.

One of the dark figures stepped up close to Bolan.

"When it is time for you to die, American, you will bless God for his mercy. Because before you die your pain will be great."

Again anger directed the terrorist's actions. His ringed fist thudded into Bolan's face and body repeatedly. His rage sated, the man finally stepped back, breathing raggedly from the effort.

"Put him inside."

Half-conscious, in a world full of pain, Mack Bolan felt himself being dragged into the rear of the 4 × 4. Doors slammed around him as he fell across the seat. The vehicle was put into gear. As it moved off across the hard, rough ground, the warrior felt every jolt. The pain kept him awake, allowed him to concentrate his mind on what lay ahead. He knew for sure that it wasn't going to be a comfortable experience. Bolan had long since accepted that discomfort came hand in hand with dedication to a cause such as his.

Like it or not, he realized he was going to have some more of the same heaped upon him in the near future.

10

By the morning of the day following Bolan's planned visit to the freight company, Jack Grimaldi was starting to get concerned. He had worked with Bolan enough times in the past to be aware of the Executioner's freewheeling way of handling missions. Bolan didn't, nor would he ever, work to a timetable. Wars couldn't be run to specific times.

But still, Bolan had promised to keep in touch, to let the flier know how things were going so he could liaise with Stony Man, and also so that Grimaldi could pass information back and forth.

Since Bolan had taken leave of him, Grimaldi had picked up Intel from Hal Brognola, courtesy of Aaron Kurtzman's computers. The Bear had been working twenty-four-hours nonstop, digging and probing, accessing data banks and crossing continents in his search for information on the dealings of Nori Hassad, the man suspected of being the Disciples' U.S. connection.

It was looking more and more like Hassad was deeply involved with the terrorists. The Bear had uncovered transactions between one of Hassad's companies and a known U.S. arms dealer. The contract had been buried deep, concealed behind numerous cover names and front companies. But Kurtzman's genius came to the fore when he latched on to a Bahamas-based export-import company he had come across once before. He knew that it was a cover for the arms dealer. Kurtzman was then able to trace the movement of cash back and forth between more than a dozen dummy accounts until he locked on to the one that belonged to Hassad. Once he had confirmed the connection, Kurtzman returned to the cash transaction's destination, and his intricate manipulation of accounts and their holders eventually produced a name known to the Stony Man information data base.

Mason Tarantino's reputation was firmly established. Arms dealers hovered between the legitimate and illegal camps. This situation was mainly due to the fact that they were used by individual groups, and sometimes by government agencies requiring covert transactions to bolster favored regimes or rebels needed to further agency actions. It was an incestuous relationship at times, not always approved, but often necessary. The twilight world of Intelligence operations existed in shadow, with the thin line between good and evil often blurred. It was all too easy to step over that line.

In Brognola's view, Tarantino had now taken that one step too far. The man's dealings with Hassad and the Disciples of Khalfi had gone beyond any acceptable demarcation zone. The man was supplying weapons and explosives that were being used against Americans on their own soil. In Brognola's eyes, there was no way Tarantino could justify this deal. Some of his semiofficial backers might try to protect him—if they were given the opportunity. The big Fed had no intention of allowing Tarantino to be spirited away by some nameless spook. The arms dealer had signed his own ticket by betraying his fellow Americans.

"I'll get this info to Striker," Grimaldi promised, "when he surfaces. Right now he's somewhere out of reach."

"When he contacts you, tell him we've covered the Chicago end. It's all buttoned down. For now. The Chicago PD is chewing the carpet because we've kept them out, and the media has been sniffing around. The shootout at the hospital has been covered as a drug-related incident. I'll keep the lid on things for as long as I can."

That had been late yesterday.

Now Grimaldi was making a low-key check on Bolan's movements. The last contact the pilot had with the Executioner had been shortly before the warrior moved out on his probe of the freight company.

Since then, nothing.

Grimaldi cruised along the highway that bypassed the freight company. The place looked normal enough, except for the fire-blackened building at the rear of the yard. Something had happened recently inside the compound, and Grimaldi felt certain Mack Bolan had been involved.

But where was he now?

The flier's keen eyes picked up the tire burns on the surface of the highway. They looked fresh. He cruised past the compound, passing the deserted diner. More tire tracks in the dust, where a vehicle had slewed off the road. Others indicated where another vehicle had rejoined the highway. Grimaldi, with nothing else to go on, followed the highway out into the open country beyond town. He drove for a few miles, searching the rolling landscape on either side of the highway.

A dirt road angled off from the highway. Grimaldi stopped his car, climbed out and examined a number of overlapping tire marks. They were all relatively fresh, the indentations of the tire treads not yet filled in by drifting dust. Which meant recent use of the dirt road.

The Stony Man flier returned to his car. He unzipped his jacket and eased out the 9 mm Beretta 92-F he was carrying. Grimaldi checked the magazine, replaced it and cocked and locked the weapon before returning it to his shoulder rig. He made sure he had the two extra magazines handy, then dropped the car into gear and wheeled it off the highway and along the dirt road.

Grimaldi studied the tracks as he drove, guessing there had to have been at least three vehicles using the road. One was an off-road type, possibly a 4×4 judging by the broad, deep-tread tire marks.

The flier knew he was assuming a great deal. The trail he followed might have nothing to do with Bolan. Grimaldi could easily end up with egg on his face. He was prepared to accept that if he was wrong. On the other hand, he had to do something, and there was a possibility he was on the right track. One way or the other he would soon find out.

If Bolan had been pursued, following his probe at the freight company, he would have had his hands full. In itself, nothing new, and Grimaldi had enough confidence in the warrior to expect him to have caused his pursuers some grief.

Easing off the gas pedal, the Stony Man pilot allowed the car to slow, then stop. He studied the way ahead, eyes reading the tracks in the dust. The lead car, probably Bolan's, had turned off the dirt road and gone down a long slope into a shallow basin. The trailing vehicles had spread out around the area before coming to a halt themselves.

Grimaldi climbed out of the car, the Beretta in his right hand. Closing the door, he walked to the top of the slope, eyes following the tire tracks that finally brought him to the dark Ford rental that Bolan had been driving when he had left the air base at Buckley. The flier studied the car for a time, checking the immediate area. There didn't appear to be anything in or around the vehicle. By "anything," Grimaldi was thinking about a body. He noticed that the driver's door was open.

Drawing his gaze back to the top of the slope, he spotted a disturbance in the dust just prior to where the car had gone over the edge. Then he spotted wide-spaced footsteps in the dust.

Grimaldi smiled to himself. Bolan had jumped from the car just before it went over the slope.

There were other footprints, too numerous to identify, but they gave Grimaldi an outline of what might have happened the previous night.

It was plain to see that Bolan had taken on his pursuers. The exact scenario was difficult to establish. All Grimaldi was able to confirm was that a firefight had taken place. He began to spot expended shell cases dotted around the area, his eye attracted by the gleaming casings lying in the dust. The pilot scouted the area, picking up a selection of the metal hulls.

There was a lot of 9 mm. He followed the scattering of casings to a cluster of rocks and brush where he located a couple of .44-caliber cases—Bolan's Desert Eagle?

There were dried blood splashes on the rock face nearby.

Bolan's blood, or his pursuers'?

Grimaldi took a slow look around, hoping to pick up some other clue that might give him an answer.

His eyes narrowed against the hard glare of the sun, the flier reached inside his jacket for the dark aviator glasses he was carrying. He was about to put them on when he caught a reflected pinpoint of light. It was off to his right, originating at the highest point of the cluster of rocks, a brief flash, moving, then holding.

Grimaldi's reflexes took over, and he dived headlong to the ground.

The crash of the single shot rattled in the pilot's ears as he hit the ground. He wriggled frantically, pressing tight against the base of a squat boulder.

The bullet struck the ground inches away from where he'd been standing.

Damn!

Grimaldi sat up, pushing back against the boulder, the Beretta gripped two-handed.

Self-preservation took over. The combat-hardened flier had been shot at too many times to treat it casually. He'd seen the end results, and there was nothing romantic or gallant about being on the receiving end of a bullet. Getting hard hit was usually the end, so the idea was *not* to stop a bullet. Let the other guy do that. First, though, it was necessary to catch him in your sights.

He eased along the boulder until he was at the far end. Twisting his body, Grimaldi lay flat and peered around the extreme edge of the boulder. By straining his eyes he was able to observe the high point where the flash of light had winked at him. Nothing showed now. The marksman was under cover, or he had already moved to a new position. Either way, it didn't help Grimaldi. He needed to know where the guy was.

What he needed was a target.

Grimaldi gathered his legs under him, casting around for a better area of cover. He saw a larger boulder ten feet away, a short enough distance under most circumstances, a long way when there was someone around equipped with a high-powered rifle.

Grimaldi sighed. Sitting on his butt waiting to be shot wasn't something he found acceptable. Because at the end of the day, the guy with the rifle wasn't about to do him any favors. If he showed up and Grimaldi was just sitting there, it made the rifleman's job a lot easier.

If the guy was on his way down he wasn't going to be moving with the rifle to his shoulder, sighting down the barrel. There had to be some odds in Grimaldi's favor.

The Stony Man flier made his decision.

He kicked himself forward, leg muscles pushing him up and forward, his attention on the distant boulder. It looked a long way off and smaller than he had first imagined. Then he shrugged the negative thoughts aside and concentrated on reaching his objective.

He had no more than three feet to cover when the slam of a shot reached his ears. The bullet hit the boulder ahead of him, skidding across the surface and leaving a pale scar. The shot came from over Grimaldi's right shoulder. He locked that thought in his mind as he launched himself forward, throwing out his left hand to break his fall as he landed on the upper face of the boulder, letting his shoulder absorb the impact. Grimaldi tucked and rolled, sliding across the surface of the rock and thumping down on his back, facing the way he'd come.

His eyes searched the rocks beyond his original hiding place—and picked up on the lean, sandy-haired figure semicrouching on a flat rock, pulling the long-barreled rifle to his shoulder as he set himself for another shot.

Grimaldi's left hand clamped around the base of the Beretta's butt, bracing his gun arm as he tracked the weapon in on the slight figure

The rifleman pulled down on his target, peering into the scope mounted on the weapon.

The flier drew breath, held it and stroked the 92-F's trigger, feeling the pistol's recoil as it fired.

The rifleman had already started his trigger pull.

Dust puffed out around the point of impact as Grimaldi's 9 mm slug punched into the target's upper chest. The impact turned the guy off balance, yet he still tried to bring his rifle back on line.

Grimaldi, pulling himself to a sitting position, triggered the Beretta twice more, spacing his shots with careful deliberation, laying them in the target's shoulder.

The rifleman fell backward, sprawling across the rock. The back of his skull impacted against the hard surface, and the rifle angled skyward, sending its shot out of harm's way before spilling from his fingers.

As Grimaldi climbed to his feet, he saw the downed man arch in a pained spasm. He crossed to where the sniper lay, reaching out to check him for weapons. He found a Smith & Wesson .45ACP Model 4506 in a shoulder holster under the man's bloodstained jacket. Grimaldi pushed the pistol under his belt, keeping the muzzle of his Beretta against the downed man's temple while he frisked him. He located the guy's wallet.

"All this just to mug me," the man whispered.

"You started it, pal," Grimaldi reminded him.

He stepped back to flip through the wallet: money, credit cards, a driver's license, giving the man's home address as Santa Fe.

"You're a long way from home," Grimaldi commented.

"I like to travel. You going to help me or what?"

"Depends."

"Always a price."

"Damn right, Becker," Grimaldi said, using the name on the driver's license. "You want to tell me who sent you?"

"I don't *want* to," Becker said, his voice drifting to a hoarse whisper. "I don't want to die, either."

"Your choice, plain and simple."

"You cops are all the same."

Grimaldi didn't put Becker right on his identity.

"We can play this game as long as you want, friend. Just remember it isn't me who's bleeding all over the place."

Becker examined his badly pulped and bleeding shoulder and chest. His face had paled and was glistening with sweat. When he looked up at Grimaldi again his eyes had trouble focusing.

"If I tell you anything I'm dead."

Grimaldi shrugged. "Die now for certain. Talk to me and maybe we help you to lose yourself."

"That straight?"

"Trust me," Grimaldi said. "I never lie."

"Yeah, I know. And Elvis is wearing a Mickey Mouse costume and working Disney World."

"Take your time, Becker. It's your blood watering the flowers. Maybe you should think about that."

"Okay, okay. Tarantino. He sent me."

"Covering his tracks?" Grimaldi said. "You mean he doesn't want to get his name in the papers next to the terrorists he's been selling to?"

"Something like that. After the shooting match last night he kind of got scared. Sent me up here to make sure there were no loose ends." Becker groaned as pain lanced through him. "Look, I need help. Man, it hurts."

"It's supposed to, Becker."

Returning to his vehicle, Grimaldi digested the information he had been given. Becker had confirmed information that Aaron Kurtzman had presented to Stony Man—that Mason Tarantino *was* involved. And running scared. If he wasn't, he wouldn't have bothered to send in one of his hired guns to mop up after Bolan's clash with the terrorists.

The only question Jack Grimaldi wanted answered now was a simple enough one.

Getting that answer was going to be the hard part.

Where was Mack Bolan?

11

The sound of a key turning in the lock drew Bolan's attention. He swung his legs off the bed and waited to see who was visiting him.

It would be his first contact with anyone since his dawn arrival at Nori Hassad's ski lodge.

The trip from his point of capture to the lodge in the mountain heights of Aspen had been hours long. Bolan, bound and hooded, had sat out the journey in silence. There was no way he could judge the mood of his captors in his condition, so he'd used the time to relax and rebuild his reserves of strength.

He was alive so far because he had something the terrorists wanted—or so they seemed to believe. If he had been little more than a nuisance, Bolan would be dead. The Disciples of Khalfi were in America because they had a mission to carry out. Taking prisoners wouldn't be on their agenda unless a captive had a use, such as providing information that might lead the terrorists to the surviving members of the news team.

But that seemed unlikely to be their motive. The terrorists appeared to be pretty well informed so far, and Bolan took the view that they wanted him more for what he knew about *their* movements. Bolan had already taken out a significant number of the Disciples. They were going to want to know who, besides Bolan, was involved.

Since his arrival they had left him alone, locked inside one of the lodge's bedrooms with an armed guard below his window and no doubt one outside the door.

That door opened now, and Bolan saw three men framed in the opening.

One, carrying a Kalashnikov AK-74, stood to one side, the muzzle of his weapon aimed directly at the warrior.

The other men entered the room, making certain that they didn't block the gunner's view of their captive.

The Executioner checked them out, making a quick decision as to the identity of the pair.

The sleek, well-dressed man would be Nori Hassad. There was no mistaking his expensive clothing, or the soft lines of his face that bore witness to his lifestyle. Good living had added pounds to his waistline and had probably blunted the hard edge of his patriotism. He was willing to give his time and money to the cause, but he would prefer to leave the dirty work to others, such as the man next to him, Bolan thought.

There was nothing soft about that one.

Bolan recognized a warrior the moment he fixed his gaze on the man.

Hard and lean, his very stance identifying him as a fighter, Rachim Gazli faced the captive his men had brought in.

After a few moment he nodded, as if confirming some inner suspicion. His eyes brightened and a trace of a cold smile edged his mouth.

He stepped farther into the room, watching Bolan closely.

"You must understand that I have not been paying close enough attention," he said, as if by way of some apology. "By that I mean that if I had, I would have realized who you were much earlier. Before I actually saw you again."

"Am I supposed to know you?" Bolan asked.

Gazli shook his head. "No. At the time you were too busy to notice me. But I remembered you and the things you did."

Hassad touched his sleeve.

"Can you be certain?" he asked.

Gazli scowled at him.

"Of course I am certain. There are things in life that you never forget. A man would have to be deaf and blind to forget this man. He may be an American, but he is also a soldier. A good soldier."

"And he is the one who has been killing our brothers?"

Gazli nodded. "This one—yes."

"He is one man, Rachim. One man."

"You are wrong. He is equal to many. You forget I have seen him in action. In Iran I saw him against many, and he alone survived. That day I realized the stories I had heard about him were true. This American who comes like a dark shadow, kills his enemies, then vanishes. And now *I* have him, Nori."

Hassad refused to meet Bolan's steely gaze. The man unnerved him. The ice-cold stare from those blue eyes seemed to burn into his very soul, stripping away the layers of flesh to expose the inner man. Hassad couldn't allow his true feelings to show, not his growing urge to surrender as he contemplated the problems surrounding the ongoing mission of the Disciples. If Gazli even imagined Hassad was thinking about quitting, he would most probably execute him on the spot. The terrorist had tunnel vision. He would keep going, attempting to complete the mission no matter what. He didn't care how many of his brothers died, just as long as he could finish the mission.

The American had the same air of dedication to *his* cause—whatever it might be. He would fight on, facing anyone who threatened his country.

Hassad was beginning to realize that he was far from being a good example for the Disciples of Khalfi, and that realization made him feel anger and shame.

His anger was directed more at himself than anyone else, due to his inability to handle the situation and its life-threatening complexities.

The shame was something Hassad would carry with him for a long time. If he survived. He knew he was letting his brothers down. Because of his inherent weakness he was placing them in danger. Despite that weakness Hassad was still a believer in the cause, which only added to his feelings of inadequacy.

While Hassad turned in on himself, Gazli appeared to be deriving satisfaction from his confrontation with Mack Bolan.

"I have heard you called by different names," he said. "What do I call you this time?"

"Does it matter?"

Gazli shrugged. "You have caused me a great deal of trouble. I should have you killed right now."

"But you won't," Bolan replied.

"Not just yet. However, that could change." Gazli moved closer, studying Bolan closely. "You understand I must ask you questions."

"Yes." Bolan turned his head to look at him. "And you understand that I'll refuse to answer them."

"So we have reached an impasse already."

Gazli turned and spoke urgently to Hassad, his voice lowered so that Bolan was unable to hear what was being said. Hassad nodded slowly, seeming relieved at being able to vacate the room.

"You leave me no choice," the terrorist said, returning to Bolan. "Believe me when I say I do not enjoy having to employ such methods. But I need to know how far we have been penetrated. How much the American authorities know about us. I will not allow you to die. When we are finished here, I, Rachim Gazli, will have you taken to Tehran to stand trial for your crimes against Islam."

"In battle a soldier fights for his cause. That is not a crime," Bolan said.

"They *are* crimes against Islam," Gazli replied, his voice rising in anger. "Your brutality knows no bounds."

"Against my enemies—yes," Bolan said. "But I don't wage war against the innocent. Or the helpless and sick in hospitals," he added pointedly.

The bitterness flooded Gazli's face now.

"It was necessary. In war there are going to be casualties. No one is ever truly innocent."

"And you aren't fighting a war in the true sense," Bolan said. "I can admire a man who stands out in the open and declares his grievances. But I have no respect for your kind. Men who skulk in the shadows and commit murder in the name of religion.''

''Believe what you wish. You cannot stop us now. There are too many of us already here. And we will complete our mission to kill the ones responsible for Ayatollah Khalfi's death. It has been decreed. We are committed.''

Bolan fell silent. He saw no point in discussing the matter with the man any longer. Harry Jordan had been right. He had told Bolan there was no compromise with these terrorists.

The one thing the terrorist leader hadn't allowed for was the fact that Mack Bolan was fired with the same determination. When it came to dealing with his enemies, the Executioner didn't quit. He refused to back down. And he never took on a mission he wasn't committed to finishing.

It had always been Bolan's way.

This time was no different.

The Disciples of Khalfi had yet to learn and understand that.

''ALL I KNOW IS he had a head-to-head with them sometime last night,'' Grimaldi said. ''The rental car is out in the mountains, but there's no sign of Striker.''

On the other end of the line Hal Brognola sighed in exasperation.

''What's your feeling, Jack?''

''Hell, I don't... Yes, I do, damn it. I think they've got him. His luck ran out and they got the drop on him.''

''Doesn't this Becker know anything?''

"He's just a triggerman for Tarantino. Like he said, he was sent in to tie up any loose ends. His capo got a case of the jitters all of a sudden. Wanted his involvement wiped off the slate."

"No way," Brognola snapped. "Tarantino has been running too close to the wind for a long time. This mess is going to take him down for good. I'll see to that myself."

"Hey, boss, that sounds personal."

"It was supposed to. Tarantino's been too greedy this time. Selling arms and explosives to a foreign assassination squad so they can kill our own people on American soil. By the time he gets out of jail I'll be retired and living in a condo on the moon."

"You sic the Feds on him?"

"Damn right. Tarantino is Most Wanted's flavor of the month."

"That still leaves us with the main players," Grimaldi said. "What about the targets?"

"The news team? Right now they're in California doing a story on the reconstruction following the last bad earthquake in L.A."

"You going to warn them about the terrorists?"

"If Striker has been compromised I might have to. Jack, you're on the spot out there. Follow up on his movements and see what you can pick up. He might need help. Keep in touch via the Farm. I'm going to head for L.A. to take charge of liaison until I know what's happening."

THERE WERE extensive cellars beneath the ski lodge. Carved out of the natural bedrock over which the lodge had been built, the cellars served as excellent storage space for the wide and varied wine stocks that Nori Hassad maintained for serving in his restaurant. Over the years he had accumulated some fine vintages from around the world, as well as wines from American sources.

At the far end of the cellar area, behind the end racks, was a concealed door that allowed entry into another storage area, which had nothing to do with Hassad's lodge business. In this secure storage area he kept another collection: armament of all shapes and sizes, ammunition for it, plus assorted weapons and equipment that might be required for the illicit activities of his Islamic brothers.

It was here, in this chill room far below the lodge, out of sight and sound of the world, that Mack Bolan found himself secured to a wooden chair and subjected to Rachim Gazli's question-and-answer session.

The terrorist leader had promised Bolan he would be kept alive until he could be transported to Tehran. He hadn't promised to keep Bolan from being hurt.

Gazli's brother Disciples were well versed in the art of interrogation. At first they used direct, physical violence, beating Bolan until he lapsed into semiconsciousness. Even Gazli himself realized this wasn't going to gain them anything. He could see that his captive would resist this kind of treatment for a long time. The terrorist leader spoke quietly with his men. One of them went away and came back carrying a portable generator unit. He set up the machine in one corner of the room and started the compact diesel engine that powered the generator. A length of electric cable, with the ends bared, was brought across to where Bolan sat.

"This can be quite effective," Gazli said conversationally, showing the Executioner the naked wires.

"Set it to low voltage," he called to the Disciple standing by the machine.

Bolan, braced as he was, arched up off the chair as Gazli touched the exposed wires to his bared left arm. The low electrical charge raced through his body, jarring nerve ends and making him gasp with agony. It felt as if his body had been kicked hard. Muscles burned as they were set rigid by the shock. Despite himself, Bolan let out a low moan, lips peeled back from his clenched teeth. When Gazli took the wires away and Bolan crashed down on the seat again, his body trembled from head to foot. His whole being ached from the tension; nerve ends screamed for relief.

"When you become used to this much power, we can increase the voltage a little at a time."

"Then you'll have to do it," Bolan said tautly. "There's not a thing I can tell you."

"I must disagree there, American. You carry knowledge inside your head that would be of great help to me. Such as how you gained information about our presence here in America. What guided you to our brothers in New York and Chicago. Who else knows about us."

"Maybe I have a crystal ball."

Gazli's jaw muscles tightened as he leaned forward, touching the wires to Bolan's arm again.

"Higher!" he commanded.

This time the shock almost tore Bolan from the chair. His body rose in a taut arch, a cry of pain barely choked back. The light before his eyes dimmed, and his entire being seemed to lose contact with reality. He was unable to gauge how long the charge ran through him. Nor was he fully aware when it ceased and his body slumped back onto the chair, sweat pouring from every pore.

"You understand the principle now. I will know when you lie, and each time you do the pain will return. The outcome is in your hands. Speak the truth, American, and you will not come to harm."

"Looks like we have a problem, then."

It took a great effort for Bolan to speak. Even his jaw muscles ached, and he had to force out each word through lips that were barely moving.

Gazli withdrew to speak with his men, leaving Bolan alone for a time. He could hear their distant voices, speaking in low, conspiratorial tones.

The warrior drew in deep breaths, trying to distance himself from the nagging pain. He pushed his thoughts away from the small room, concentrating on definite images, something that he could latch on to, anything that would detach him from the pain. When it came, he wasn't surprised to find the face of Barbara Price floating before him.

Bolan channeled every conscious thought toward retaining that image, cutting himself off from his immediate surroundings, distancing himself from the hurt in his body. The image of the woman was in direct contrast to the starkness of his situation. *She* was normality, stability, a breath of freshness in a world of hurt. She was someone Bolan cared for, his anchor of calm in a grim ocean of chaos. In his mind he reached out to touch her, and for a moment his pain drifted away, leaving him free and clear from the horror of reality.

The cold water, thrown into his face, jerked Bolan back with a shock. He opened his eyes and stared up at Gazli. The terrorist leader was smiling at him.

"No time for dreaming, American," he said. "We´ have to begin again."

And so it went on, the questions followed by more jolting shocks from the electric cable when Bolan refused to answer.

Questions, pain, questions, pain.

Bolan was thrown completely out of synch. His mind and body lost all touch with real time. He found he was unable to work out the simplest fact. He couldn't figure whether it was day or night, or how long he had been held in the lodge's cellar.

All he knew was Gazli's droning voice and the pain that followed. They were the only real things in his world, the only points he could associate.

Gazli's voice meant pain, pain became Gazli.

The two were one, and they were endless, until Bolan no longer cared, or fought. His ravaged body reacted to the electric shocks, but the dulled nerves within him had no reserves left.

He lay slumped in the chair, trying to retain the fading image of Barbara Price's lovely face. It came and went now, drifting in and out of the foggy shadows obscuring it, and Bolan had to dredge up fragments of conscious thought in order to preserve that image. If she vanished, he would have nothing left.

In the end, he did keep that image before him, locking on to it with grim determination, shutting out everything else.

And it seemed to be working, because Bolan didn't register any more shocks. He simply lay in a deep stupor, not fully aware of anything around him. He would drift into semiconsciousness for periods, then float back to the surface.

GRIMALDI WAS AIRBORNE. He flew Dragon Slayer across country, checking his charts as he piloted the helicopter. He was doing what he always did when the odds were going against him—he was going on instinct, and Jack Grimaldi's instinct told him to check out Nori Hassad's ski lodge. He recalled Bolan's references to the lodge on more than one occasion. Plus the fact that the freight company in Boulder had been owned by the guy. A pessimist would say they were simply coincidences. As far as Grimaldi was concerned, they were too much like coincidences, and there had to be some mileage in checking them out.

He sighted the Aspen airport configuration below. Grimaldi contacted air control, verified his earlier flight plan and requested a touchdown point. He was directed to a corner of the field and put the combat chopper down on a helicopter pad.

Once he had checked in and been given clearance, Grimaldi made his way to one of the rental counters within the terminal building. He rented a Cherokee 4×4, threw his bag on the rear seat and headed out of the airport.

The day was bright and clear, the air warm. Grimaldi checked his location on the area map provided by the rental company. It took him no more than a few minutes to pinpoint Hassad's ski lodge. It lay higher up the mountain slopes than the old silver town of Aspen, snug in the rocky folds of the Elk Mountains. Dust trailed in the wake of the 4×4 as Grimaldi wound his way through Roaring Fork Valley, gunning the Cherokee along the winding road. Above Grimaldi, the green sward of pines layered the majestic mountain slopes, devoid in the summer heat of the white snow mantle that drew the crowds during the skiing season.

Grimaldi opened the window on his door, allowing the pine-scented air to infiltrate the driving compartment. He was traveling along a stretch of road that tunneled through high slopes thick with close-ranked pines. Fragmented sunlight lanced down from the intertwined canopy formed by the tall trees, the pale shafts alive with swirling dust motes. Occasionally Grimaldi was able to pick out patches of the empty blue sky.

He emerged from the natural tunnel some miles later, taking the 4×4 around a gentle curve that hugged the side of a high rock slope. On the other side the land fell away in a series of sculptured steps. Bare, weathered rock and loose shale slopes were dotted with hardy grasses and wildflowers.

Another twenty minutes brought Grimaldi to the cutoff that marked the entrance to the ski lodge's access road. He eased the Cherokee to a stop and sat studying the area for a time. A publicity brochure he'd read said the lodge was a mile farther up the side of the mountain.

There was no reason to drive up to the lodge, he decided. If his suspicions were correct and the Disciples of Khalfi were in residence, there was no point advertising his presence.

Reversing the 4×4 into cover beside the road, Grimaldi exited the vehicle and pushed into the pine stands edging the access road. The trees would provide cover, and the thick carpet of pine needles deadened the sound of his passing. Grimaldi kept the access road in sight as he progressed up the ever-rising terrain. The tree cover shielded him from the direct glare of the sun, but the dense growth of trees and foliage contained the heat, creating a scented hothouse effect.

The Stony Man pilot was making good progress, closing in on the lodge when he heard the distant sound of a car approaching. He moved closer to the road, staying under cover behind a thick trunk, and spotted the Chrysler as it rounded a bend. It passed him quickly, and, being on a higher level than the road, Grimaldi was unable to see inside the vehicle. All he could do was watch it roll out of sight, the sound of the engine fading.

12

The warmth of sunlight on Bolan's face alerted him to a change in his surroundings. He moved, realizing he was no longer strapped in the chair. He was lying down on a soft surface, and after a while he realized he was on a bed. When he opened his eyes he saw that he was back in the room he had occupied earlier.

The moment Bolan tried to move, his abused body shrieked in silent protest. The prolonged electric-shock treatment had left him stiff and aching. He felt as if he were suffering from extreme burn, resulting from relentless exercise. His muscles had almost seized up. Bolan refused to give in to the condition. He forced himself into a sitting position, panting from the effort, his body under the blacksuit damp with sweat. Greater effort and control was required to get him on his feet and across the room, dragging his heavy feet with each step. He forced himself to complete a number of circuits, loosening the tensed muscles and getting the blood to circulate around his system.

He was on his ninth circuit when he heard a sound outside his window. Bolan pressed against the wall to one side of the glass, enabling himself to look down to the area in front of the lodge.

A blue Chrysler was parked on the graveled driveway. The trunk was open, and one of the terrorists was loading it. He placed a couple of suitcases inside, then a pair of aluminum cases, similar to the kind used by photographers to house equipment. He laid them side by side, covering them with a couple of thick blankets before shutting and locking the trunk.

Bolan didn't believe for one minute that the cases contained cameras. He was recalling body harnesses containing explosive devices and detonators.

Gazli appeared. He was dressed for travel, in lightweight clothing, as were the three men who accompanied him. Hassad trailed behind, standing to one side as Gazli and his companions exchanged words with the men remaining behind. It was obvious from the way they were bidding one another goodbye that the terrorist leader was about to do something important. Their manner was intense as they embraced and shook hands.

Bolan memorized the license plate of the car.

Gazli's men climbed into the car, leaving the terrorist leader to say a few words to Hassad, who nodded, taking Gazli's hand briefly before the Disciples' leader climbed behind the steering wheel and drove away from the lodge. Bolan watched it roll down the drive until it vanished from sight.

The Executioner's guess was that Gazli and his men were on the way to complete their mission. They had located the surviving members of the news team and were setting out to assassinate them.

Bolan moved away from the window as the armed guard returned to his former position watching over the lodge. Hassad and the two remaining Disciples went back inside the building. Counting the gunner outside his door, Bolan figured he had at least five hardmen to deal with, unless there were others inside the lodge he wasn't aware of.

Before he need worry about those, Bolan realized, he had to get out of his room and arm himself.

He made a quick circuit of the room, checking out its contents for anything he could use as a means of distraction. He had to draw the guard from the corridor into the room. It didn't take long for Bolan to realize there was little he could utilize. The room had been stripped of anything that might be useful as a weapon. Apart from the bed, there was nothing portable in the place. Gazli had made sure there was no means for his captive to construct any kind of offensive weaponry. Even the adjoining bathroom was devoid of anything but the standard built-in items.

Back in the bedroom, Bolan sat on the edge of the bed, staring at the wide, panoramic window overlooking the drive.

There had to be something he could use.

He pushed to his feet in frustration. The sudden action dislodged the bed, moving it a few inches across the carpet. Bolan dropped to his knees, peering under the bed. It wasn't fixed to the floor. It sat on casters.

Bolan peeled the sheets and mattress off the base, upended the bed and slid it across the floor until it was positioned at the window.

There was no guarantee this would have the effect he wanted. On the other hand, if he didn't try, he was going to have to sit and wait for something else to come along. And that might be too late for the unsuspecting members of the news team.

With his decision made, Bolan crouched and took hold of the bed's corner. He lifted and tilted it at the same time, aiming the bed at the wide pane of glass. He was helped by the fact that the window had a low sill. The bed base toppled forward, hit and shattered the glass, then dropped through the frame.

GRIMALDI SPRINTED for the cover of the lodge wall, then headed for the service door.

Trying the door, he found that it was unlocked. He slipped inside and found he was just off the lodge's spacious kitchen area.

The gleaming kitchen equipment was cold and unused. Only a single coffeepot was working, blowing spirals of steam into the air.

Somewhere within the lodge Grimaldi heard raised voices. Doors slammed, followed by the clatter of running feet.

He proceeded farther into the building, moving from the kitchen to the main restaurant. The tables were bare and chairs had been upended on them. Through a wide, sweeping, panoramic window, the Stony Man pilot had a majestic view of soaring mountain peaks, swathed in greenery, merging with the blue sky on the far, hazy horizon.

THE MOMENT the glass shattered, Bolan turned and crossed the room, flattening himself against the wall on the hinge side of the door. He picked up the click of the lock turning and braced himself as the door swung inward.

The armed guard took a cautious step into the room.

Bolan, behind the opened door, let precious seconds tick away. He wanted the guard a little farther inside before he made his move. But he also knew that the longer he waited, the greater the odds against his succeeding.

From below the shattered window the outside guard gave an angry yell. Bolan couldn't understand what he was saying, but his words prompted the guy behind the door to push farther into the room, the muzzle of his AK-74 tracking ahead of him.

The moment the guard's head and shoulders eased into view, Bolan threw his whole weight against the door. It slammed against the guard's left side, angling the muzzle of the assault rifle toward the far wall.

Making the most of his opportunity, Bolan reached out and caught hold of the guard's left wrist, twisting it hard against the joint. The man spit air from between his clenched teeth, struggling to free himself. His resistance only increased the unnatural turn of his arm, giving him more pain.

As Bolan moved fully into view, the guard tried to bring his rifle around one-handed, but his attempt was too slow. The Executioner delivered a brutal elbow smash to the side of his adversary's head and neck, driving him up against the wall. Still twisting on the man's left arm, Bolan forced the guy to double over. The guard's lowering head and Bolan's rising knee connected with devastating force. Crushed flesh spurted bright blood. The guard slumped back against the wall, his face a glistening mask of red. Bolan stepped in close and drove the heel of his right palm up under the guard's exposed jaw. The impact smashed the terrorist's mouth shut with crushing force. The sudden pressure snapped the guard's head back, slamming the back of his skull against the wall. The guard went down as if his legs had been cut from beneath him.

The warrior grabbed the Kalashnikov, making a quick check of the magazine. He switched the selector to single shot, then crouched beside the downed guard and frisked him. He found a second magazine tucked into the man's waistband. Bolan took it and slipped it into one of his blacksuit pockets. The guard had no other weapons.

Straightening, Bolan crossed the room and edged to the window frame. The guard below was just moving back into view from one side of the driveway, and he raised his weapon as he caught a glimpse of movement.

The Executioner didn't hesitate. He leaned out and triggered two closely spaced shots from the AK-74. The pair of 5.45 mm steel-cored hollowpoints punched into the moving terrorist. They drove through his chest cavity, the tumbling action of the deformed slugs expanding the internal damage. The man stumbled and fell, his own weapon spilling from his fingers as he hit the ground in a rolling tangle of arms and legs.

Stepping over the low sill, Bolan eased himself onto the angled porch roof that ran the length of the lodge. Leaning in against the upright section, he moved forward until he was able to scramble up onto the low-pitched roof. He hugged the surface, sprinting to its apex, then down the other side. He reached the far side of the building, moving from level to level until he was able to drop to the ground at the rear of the lodge. From there Bolan was able to cut across a patch of open ground to the cover of a nearby stand of pine trees.

TWO CLOSELY SPACED SHOTS had reached Grimaldi's ears shortly after he entered the lodge. They came from overhead, filtering down from somewhere inside the building.

Minutes later he heard more gunfire, outside the lodge this time, rapid autofire.

Then silence.

Grimaldi left the restaurant behind. He was in a large, low-ceilinged room fitted out as a lounge bar.

He had taken no more than a couple of steps across the carpeted floor when a rustle of sound alerted him. Someone's noisy intake of breath indicated a moment of physical effort.

Grimaldi ducked, breaking to one side, and turned.

He caught a glimpse of a round-faced, sweating man, halfway through swinging a heavy bottle at Grimaldi's head. The flier was easily able to avoid the clumsy blow. He stepped under the slow-moving arm, driving his left fist deep into the attacker's soft belly. The guy grunted and fell back. Grimaldi straightened, bringing the Beretta around in a clubbing arc that connected with his adversary's exposed jawline. The hard steel crunched against soft flesh. The attacker staggered away from Grimaldi, colliding with the bar, the bottle flying from his hand and rolling across the carpet. He hung where he was for a moment, eyes glazing over, before crashing to the floor with a heavy thump.

A BULLET hitting the trunk of one of the trees alerted Bolan to the fact that he had been spotted. Wood splinters filled the air around him as he ducked and went for cover.

Now he could hear sounds of pursuit.

The rattle of an AK-74 on full-auto ripped through the crisp air. Bullets chopped and chewed into the foliage, whipping at low branches, shredding bark from the sturdy trunks.

Bolan peered through the foliage, separating movement from shadow, watching for the substance, not the tricks of light.

The seconds ticked away as the warrior played the waiting game, something he was familiar with. During his tours of Vietnam, he had perfected his technique, blending into his surroundings and waiting for the enemy to come to him.

The Kalashnikov was already at his shoulder, requiring only the slightest move to put it on target.

He waited and allowed his adversaries to walk into his field of fire.

There were two of them within sight, moving close together instead of spacing themselves apart.

Whatever else they might be, these Disciples of Khalfi were no jungle fighters. They preferred the urban jungle, cities and back alleys, sniping from the cover of solid buildings or from moving cars.

They were out of their own killing grounds now and in the Executioner's.

And sentence had been passed.

The AK-74 cracked twice, paused, then fired twice more. The terrorists were slammed to the ground in an instant, head shots delivering them from daylight to eternal night in the space of a heartbeat.

Bolan was already on the move, circling the pair and returning to the edge of the tree line, yards away from where he had entered it. Concealed beneath overhanging foliage, the warrior studied the ski lodge, watching for sound or movement before slipping from the shadows and closing on the rear of the building.

TWO SHOTS RANG OUT, followed a split second later by two more.

Grimaldi walked through the lounge and saw sliding glass doors that led outside. He kept out of sight, pressing against the wall, as he neared the doors.

Almost there, he sensed movement on the other side of the glass.

The door slid aside on silent roller, and Grimaldi caught a glimpse of a gun barrel, recognizing it as a Kalashnikov AK-74 assault rifle.

He waited long enough for the intruder to step inside, and as the figure drew level Grimaldi lifted the Beretta and pressed the muzzle against the man's head.

BOLAN REACHED the large sliding glass doors. No sound came from inside the room on the other side of the glass. He checked it out, discovering it was one of the lodge's lounges. It was empty now, and he slid open one of the glass doors.

The warrior took a cautious step inside, the muzzle of the assault rifle tracking ahead, his eyes searching.

A flicker of movement off to the right caught the warrior's attention, and he began to turn—only to feel the cold steel ring of a pistol muzzle press against the side of his head.

13

Jack Grimaldi felt a sliver of ice skate the length of his spine as he recognized the intruder. His finger eased away from the Beretta's trigger, and he let out a deep breath.

"Thanks for the warm welcome, Jack," Bolan said dryly. "I'll remember to do the same for you one day."

The pilot sagged back against the wall, his gun drooping floorward.

"Do you have to go creeping around like that?"

"What's the situation in here?" the Executioner asked.

"I came across only one hostile. He's back there taking a break. I take it you handled the rest?"

Bolan inclined his head as he moved past his friend.

"Is he alive?"

"Yeah. Son of a bitch tried to deck me with a bottle."

Grimaldi followed Bolan through the lounge until they came across Hassad's sprawled form. The man was still spread-eagled on the floor. Blood from his badly cut jaw had stained the expensive carpet around his head. Kneeling, Bolan turned Hassad onto his back.

"He doesn't look like your usual terrorist," Grimaldi commented. "He'd lose breath running for the phone."

"It's an educated guess, but I'd say we've got the local organizer for the Disciples."

"Hassad?"

Bolan nodded. "Expensive clothes, gold watch, handmade shoes. This guy hasn't seen the streets of the Middle East for a long time, Jack. He was with the hit team earlier. From what I heard he isn't too happy about getting involved in the dirty end of the business."

"He's been a capitalist for too long. Enjoys the good life."

"That's over for him now," Bolan said. "My worry is the hit team. They took off in a hurry some time ago. I need to know where they were headed."

"A car passed me on my way up here. You figure they're on their way to make a hit?"

"Yeah, I'm sure of it. What we need to know is where."

"Hal got a line on the news team. They're in Los Angeles filming a report. He's on his way there now."

"Jack, get Hassad on his feet and able to talk. We need to ask him a few questions before I call up Stony Man."

Bolan made his way across the lounge. He continued on until he emerged in the lodge's spacious reception area. The quiet calm of the place made him realize how hectic his own time had been over the past few days. He seemed to have been on the move nonstop since starting out on the mission. New York, the jumping off point, felt a hundred years away.

A paneled door led Bolan into a large, expensively appointed office. Three telephones stood on a huge, polished wood desk. Nearby, a percolator bubbled away on a small table, sending the rich aroma of coffee into the air. Bolan took a moment to pour himself a china mug of the black brew before slumping into the padded leather executive chair behind the desk. He placed the AK-74 on the desk top and stared across the expansive room.

Inactivity brought a feeling of lethargy. As his body relaxed, it accepted that Bolan had been pushing it to the limit, exceeding the resources it stored, not in unlimited quantities, but the normal amounts of any human being. Mack Bolan was mortal, though there were those around him, both friend and foe, who might believe otherwise. His capacity for taking himself beyond the limits acted as a stimulant to those who fought alongside him, spurring them on to drive their own frail forms to carry out acts of courage and dedication they might otherwise back away from. Bolan's drive and resourcefulness worked almost like a weapon against those he confronted as enemies. His seeming indestructibility had turned his adversaries away from him, instilling fear and weakness when they were faced with his fighting skills.

But Bolan the man would never have attested to those qualities. He did what he had to do in the face of overwhelming odds, and did it with no regard to his own benefit or aggrandizement.

The door opened, breaking the moment of calm, and Bolan sat upright as Grimaldi brought Nori Hassad into the room. The Stony Man pilot pushed the dazed man before him, guiding him to a chair.

Hassad, still bleeding from the gash on his cheek, stared at Bolan with naked fear in his eyes. He found it difficult to comprehend the man. Only a short time earlier this American had been a prisoner, being subjected to physical torture of the most base kind. Now he was free, and the Disciples left behind to watch him were dead.

Draining the coffee mug, Bolan leaned forward and looked at Hassad. The warrior's battered face, still showing the marks of the torture he had received, made him all the more formidable.

"How does it feel to be on your own, Hassad? Without your friends around to protect you?"

Hassad curled up inside. He held Bolan's gaze but didn't speak, because he had no words for this man.

"You realize it's all over? All that you've built up is gone. All you have to look forward to is a jail cell. For a long time."

"It'll be a pretty uncomfortable stay," Grimaldi said from where he stood at Hassad's side, "in among all those hard timers. Nice soft guy like you, Hassad. They'll use you, my friend, and it won't be nice."

"You cannot frighten me," Hassad blurted. "I will claim . . . asylum."

"A terrorist? Working against the country that allowed him to come in and build his business?" Bolan stated. "Hassad, we have all the proof we need. Harboring known terrorists. Aiding in the purchase of illegal weapons and explosives. Allowing business premises to be used in the manufacture of devices intended to kill U.S. citizens."

"You cannot do this," Hassad protested. "I am . . . I . . ."

"I know what you are, Hassad, and there's no way you'll walk away from this."

"God will protect me from the American government."

Bolan stood. "But can He protect you from *me?*"

"What do you mean?"

"Right now you're in my hands. The government doesn't tell me what to do. I make my own decisions."

"What do you want?"

"You know what I want. Rachim Gazli. What does he intend to do in Los Angeles?"

Hassad's head rose, eyes searching Bolan's stone face.

"How did . . . ?"

Bolan looked across the top of Hassad's head to where Grimaldi stood. The flier gave a brief smile.

"We know more than you realize," the warrior stated. "We know Gazli has gone to Los Angeles to assassinate the surviving members of the news team, the ones you claim were instrumental in the death of Ayatollah Khalfi. Which you also know is not true."

"They provoked the attack on Khalfi."

"No. That was an internal matter between your own factions. And now it's being used as an excuse to terrorize and murder innocent Americans."

"The decision has been made. It is the responsibility of the Americans. Khalfi is dead. His honor must be—"

"Don't talk to me about honor," Bolan growled. "There's no honor in slaughter, no glory in the indiscriminate murder of people who had no part in this matter. Hassad, you people are using America to cover up internal strife within your group, blaming someone else because the intolerance you crow about is not ours but your own.''

Hassad shook his head, anger and the pain from his battered face adding to his confusion. He felt trapped, with no way out. His fear created wild imaginings, and for some strange reason he thought about the torture that Gazli had subjected this man to. If the Americans did the same to him, there was no way he wouldn't talk. Despite himself, he would tell them everything they wanted to know just to avoid being hurt. The imagined threat took control and gave Hassad a strength he could never have summoned under normal circumstances.

Without warning he lunged from the chair, hurling himself at Grimaldi. Hassad's bulk propeled the pair across the room. They collided with a wooden card table, the piece of furniture collapsing under their combined weight. Hassad was screaming wildly, his rage and fear adding volume to his outburst. He lashed out with clenched fists, catching Grimaldi across the side of the head, more by good luck than judgment. As the flier rolled to one side, trying to avoid his adversary's blows, he felt the man's hands clawing at his holstered pistol. His response was a fraction slow, and he felt the weapon slip free from its holster.

''He's got my gun!'' Grimaldi yelled, warning Bolan.

Hassad rolled across the carpet, crashing against the wall. He struggled to gain his feet, fumbling to free the safety on the Beretta 92-F.

''Put the gun down, Hassad!''

Bolan's voice snapped him back to reality. He saw the tall, black-clad American coming around the desk, armed with the AK-74 that had been lying on the desk.

"What will you do? Kill me?"

"If you make me."

Hassad smiled. It was almost a smile of triumph.

"No, this is one kill you will not take credit for. Nor will you torture me so I betray my brothers."

Nori Hassad turned the Beretta on himself. He jammed the muzzle between his lips, angling it toward the roof of his mouth, and pulled the trigger. The muffled crack of the shot was followed by a gout of red that erupted from the top of his shattered skull. Hassad's body stiffened, arching violently as he fell back against the wall and toppled to the carpeted floor.

He was dead by the time Bolan and Grimaldi reached him.

14

Rachim Gazli watched the landscape roll by without really seeing it. His thoughts were absorbed by the complications of the the mission, especially the coming phase, which, if it went well, would mean the completion of his operation in the United States.

This part had to go well.

Too many things had gone sour over the past few days due to the interference of the American. The man had to be admired for his persistence and fighting skills, but Gazli held only anger for what he had done to the Disciples of Khalfi. The men he had lost were part of himself. Their deaths were felt deeply. It was as if Gazli had lost a piece of his own being with each brother taken from him. His only consolation was that they would receive their reward in paradise.

It placed a greater burden on his shoulders. The loss of his comrades, before they had completed their mission, meant he had to ensure success. It was for him to snatch victory from the bloody hands of the Americans, to show them how vulnerable they were even within the borders of their own nation. America had to learn that she wasn't invincible, that retribution came to all. The first lesson would be the destruction of the men responsible for Ayatollah Khalfi's death.

America would read with shock how they died, and Islam would be avenged.

Gazli leaned forward and picked up the telephone Hassad had fitted to his expensive automobile. He punched in the number and waited.

When it was answered, Gazli spoke in his own tongue.

"Jaffir, we are on our way."

Gazli's Los Angeles contact man, Jaffir Khalil, acknowledged with good news.

"Everything is prepared. We have confirmed the location. And I have a way you can get in. All will be ready when you arrive."

"Good. Has the expected consignment arrived?"

"Yes. The delivery was successful. We will be able to begin distribution within the next day or so."

"Excellent, Jaffir. Now do you have somewhere we can rest until the time to strike?"

"Yes. Meet me at the rendezvous point and I will take you there."

"If we keep to the schedule, I will be with you by midmorning tomorrow."

"Very well, Rachim. Contact me again when you reach the city. Until tomorrow."

Gazli replaced the receiver and settled back in the luxury of the comfortable seat.

"Is everything all right?" one of his companions asked.

"Yes, Salim, everything is very well. Very well indeed."

Gazli closed his eyes, allowing the rhythm of the car to lull him. He turned his mind to thoughts of the American warrior. There would be double pleasure in store if Gazli was able to complete the strike against the guilty journalists *and* bring the warrior back to Tehran to stand trial for his crimes against Islam. He regretted not being able to complete his interrogation of the man. He would have been happier if he had learned what the man carried in his head. Although the American appeared to operate alone, he had to have some higher authority he was answerable to. There had to be a chain of command. The man would need an intelligence source to feed him information. Otherwise, how would he have learned of the Disciples' presence in the United States?

It would have been useful to uncover details of that source, to learn how the man's organization operated. It would have been a genuine coup, one that would have benefited Gazli's superiors. He shrugged the matter aside. He had almost forgotten that there would yet be an opportunity to interrogate the American further. Once the man was in Tehran, Gazli's people would be able to interrogate him for as long as they liked, and use methods guaranteed to extract information.

The fact that Gazli hadn't established how much the Americans knew about his presence in the country troubled him to a degree. It would have eased the situation to understand more, but sometimes in the midst of a war it was necessary to operate under extreme conditions. Gazli accepted that. He and his men were capable of facing whatever the Americans put in their path. If they did have to die, with their mission completed or not, the Disciples of Khalfi were prepared physically and spiritually. And with the weaponry carried in the trunk of the car, they would take a great many Americans with them on their journey to paradise.

THEY DROVE through the rest of the day and the night that followed. Stops were made only to refuel the car and stretch their legs. They chose isolated gas stations, making their fuel purchases quietly and without fuss. Gazli wanted to make the journey to Los Angeles without alerting anyone. Drawing attention to themselves would only put the American authorities on their guard.

To ensure they kept on the move, Gazli rotated his men, giving each of them a two-hour stretch behind the wheel. As there were four of them in the car, it was a simple enough equation to operate. Whenever they passed through a town, they would stop at fast-food establishments to purchase hot coffee and food to keep themselves refreshed. Gazli found the food bland and almost uneatable, but at least the coffee was strong and helped to keep them awake.

He kept the radio on, listening to news items in case there was any mention of the Disciples. He didn't expect the American authorities would release such information willingly. On the other hand, he was aware of the independent nature of the American media. If they learned of the Disciples presence in the country they might well broadcast the news. But there was nothing. Gazli had listened to earlier radio and television reports while on the move and also at the ski lodge. Nothing had been forthcoming even then. The

Americans appeared to be keeping the whole affair under cover in case such news panicked the population, which was, after all, made up of nothing more than self-indulgent weaklings, fed watered-down bulletins and endless junk programs to keep their dulled brains slumbering.

BY MIDMORNING Gazli, taking his turn behind the wheel, drove through the outskirts of Los Angeles. He consulted the highway signs, following the directions that Khalil had provided when he had called him to confirm their arrival.

The many-laned freeway was choked with vehicles. The warm air shimmered with the exhaust fumes from thousands of cars moving at a walking pace. Gazli closed his mind to the extremes of human existence and allowed his thoughts to be captured by matters of greater importance. The initial strike against the American media in Los Angeles was no more than a prelude to a wider campaign against the Western world on a global scale. The Disciples of Khalfi were going to spearhead more assassinations and sabotage, all intended to right the wrongs perpetrated against Islam. He and his brothers were tired of the rhetoric, the half promises, the lies, the heel-dragging of the politicians. They wanted justice, an equalizing of the balance between the followers of Islam and the disbelievers, an accounting. And they would have it, once the world saw what a small but dedicated group could do if they were carried by faith.

America was going to bleed and burn, and the world would tremble when it became aware that America was only the first to feel the wrath of the Disciples.

Following the signs, Gazli eventually picked up the Santa Monica Freeway. He followed it toward the coast, taking the off ramp for Santa Monica Pier, and eventually pulled into one of the parking lots. The area was busy with tourists flocking around the shops and restaurants. There were ample crowds, enough people so that Gazli and his three companions didn't stand out. They had changed earlier into lightweight, casual clothing, carrying cameras around their necks, so there was little to distinguish them from the dozens of other visitors.

Gazli wandered across to one of the shops, pausing outside to examine the racks of postcards of the area.

After a minute Jaffir Khalil appeared at his side. The two men exchanged glances, then Khalil moved on. Gazli followed after a moment, and they fell in step.

"Your journey was uneventful?" Khalil asked.

"There were no problems."

"Good. I have a car nearby. We will transfer your belongings, then I will take you to the house. Saleem will remove your vehicle and dispose of it."

"He will make certain to be thorough?"

"Don't worry, my brother. Saleem understands what has to be done. It may be unnecessary, but it is a wise precaution in case the police are looking for it."

"It was unfortunate I was unable to spend more time with the American we captured. I am convinced he has information about us. How much and who he shares it with is not known."

"Once you have him in Tehran, time will be on your side. You will be able to learn everything he knows."

"Be assured of that, Jaffir. He has much to answer for. But he will fail in trying to stop me from completing my mission. Now that we are this far and so close, nothing will prevent me from destroying the members of that news team."

"All is arranged."

"Is the time the same?"

"Tomorrow evening."

"You have done well, Jaffir, my brother."

They were crossing the parking lot and Khalil raised a casual hand, alerting the driver of his waiting vehicle. He and Gazli continued on as the parked car, a nondescript gray sedan, eased out of its slot and rolled along the lane behind them.

"Here," Gazli said.

He opened the trunk and lifted out the luggage and the two aluminum cases. They were transferred to the trunk of the sedan as it pulled to a halt. Khalil's driver slid out from behind the wheel and took over the terrorist leader's vehicle. Gazli's three companions were already out of the car and climbing into the sedan.

Gazli slid in beside Khalil as he took the wheel. Seconds later they were moving off, slipping in behind a Toyota filled with rowdy children. The kids in the rear of the Toyota waved at Gazli, making faces at him, and he waved back, smiling, as well. The children were unaware that the smile went no further than his mouth. The man's eyes were cold and empty. At the exit, the Toyota turned right. Khalil eased into the left hand lane, driving steadily. He seemed completely at ease with the never-ending streams of moving vehicles that clogged the road.

"This is a mad place," one of the Iranian's observed quietly from the back seat of the sedan. "So many cars. All hurrying about. Do these Americans never stop?"

"Only when they sleep," Khalil informed him. "Americans do everything in a hurry. Life is one long race for them."

"But where are they going?"

He shrugged. "Ask them and they do not know."

"Tomorrow we will help some of them to find out."

"Jaffir, I still feel uneasy about the car," Gazli said. "Does Saleem understand it must be completely destroyed?"

Khalil nodded. "Be at peace, my brother. Saleem will not let us down."

FOR SALEEM THE DAY had started well, and promised to continue in that vein. He felt honored to be assigned to the task of destroying the car Rachim Gazli had traveled in. He was one of the youngest of Jaffir Khalil's group. He had lived in America for more than three years and blended in well. His Islamic background was known, but he had never publicly acknowledged any affiliation with extremist groups, or even voiced any opinions. He worked in his grandfather's grocery store in East L.A., had many friends of varying nationalities within the local communities and had never been in trouble with the law. Outwardly Saleem was a friendly young man trying to make his way in a tough world.

Behind the facade was a dedicated Islamic fundamentalist, just waiting for the day when he could demonstrate his loyalty to the cause. That day had come, and Saleem was determined to prove himself.

His day began to go wrong after he had left the Santa Monica Freeway, turned off onto the Harbor Freeway and drove down as far as the junction with Firestone Boulevard. From Firestone he was able to cut across into the Watts District, where he had a date with some acquaintances who were going to help him get rid of the car. That was the only part of the plan of which he had failed to inform Kahlil. He had met the people he'd hired in a local bar, and Saleem knew they were involved in the auto business—perhaps not legally, but they did have the right connections when it came to disposing of vehicles. Saleem had made a bargain with them, using the money Khalil had supplied for his part in the operation. He had simply not gone into detail about how the car would be disposed of, and Khalil, who had always depended on the young Disciple, saw no reason to question him further.

He turned the car into a narrow, trash-strewn alley between two long-abandoned buildings and spotted the black panel truck belonging to his friends. He braked the car to a stop and climbed out.

He saw the three young men waiting beside the truck, eyeing the car as Saleem approached them.

"Hey, Sal, you made it."

Dino was the leader of the three. Thin-faced, with a scrawny beard and small, mean eyes, he fancied himself a hardman. Lean to the point of being almost skeletal, Dino Marchetti was an opportunist who never passed up anything that might net him a dollar. Now, as he cast his greedy gaze over the sleek, expensive lines of the Chrysler, his mind was busily working out the profit he could make on a deal for the car.

"Is everything set?" Saleem asked.

Dino, still calculating, didn't answer immediately. He was already working out his cut if he took the car to a guy he knew. The man had a thriving business in handling stolen vehicles. He had the organization to change identity and appearance within a few hours. His deals were always for cash, and Dino, who was a regular, received top dollar.

"Dino?"

Saleem began to feel a little uneasy. He wasn't sure why until Dino opened the driver's door and began to inspect the car's interior.

"Low mileage," Dino said, almost to himself. "Clean inside. No sweat making a deal for this."

Saleem stepped up behind Dino, reaching out to drop his hand on the man's skinny shoulder.

"What are you taking about, Dino? Our deal is for totaling the car. Remember?"

Dino straightened, his head turning so he could stare at Saleem.

"Hey, man, don't make a fuss. I'm still going to get rid of it. Nobody's going to recognize this set of wheels when it gets back on the road. Even its owner wouldn't know it."

Saleem felt a cold chill settle in the pit of his stomach. This wasn't how he had arranged things. It had to be the way Khalil wanted. Nothing else was acceptable.

"You don't understand, Dino. The car *has* to be destroyed. Completely. No trace. We agreed. I paid you up front."

Dino managed a death's-head grin.

"Hey, you're right there, Sal. I almost forgot. The way I see it, I'm getting paid twice. It must be my birthday."

Saleem realized he was losing it. The deal was going badly wrong. If Dino insisted on changing things, it could endanger the whole of the Disciples' mission. And he couldn't allow that to happen.

"Look, forget it, Dino. Hey, you keep the money, and I'll lose the car myself."

Dino's smile almost convinced Saleem. He felt confident enough to turn back toward the car.

He had almost reached it when he heard the soft scuff of footsteps behind him. As he turned, something struck him across the back of the skull, and pain exploded inside his head. Saleem stumbled and fell to his knees, dazed. He could feel blood trickling down the back of his neck, under the collar of his shirt. Rough hands grabbed hold of his arms. Fingers knotted themselves in his hair and his head was yanked back. Dino's face swam into view. He wasn't smiling now.

"Stupid mother!" Dino said very softly, shaking his head. "You think I'm going to let you drive away with that car? You realize how much I can get for it? And you want me to total it."

"We made a deal—"

"Uh-uh, asshole. I took your money, is all. You know what else? I ain't givin' it back."

Dino's right hand appeared before Saleem's eyes. He saw in a moment of stomach-churning clarity that the man was holding a slim-bladed knife.

The tough leaned forward. The knife hand vanished from Saleem's sight, and a split second later he felt sharp pain slide from one side of his throat to the other. After a moment of numbness the pain returned, stronger this time, and Saleem screamed. The sound came out as a bubbling rattle because blood was seeping into his throat from the terrible gash in his flesh. As the shock of the gaping wound began to register, Saleem began to jerk and squirm, blood pumping in streams from severed arteries. It soaked the front of his shirt all the way down to his waist. Saleem would have fallen if Dino's two partners hadn't been holding him upright, and they maintained their grip until the young man's death throes had ceased.

"You going to stand there all goddamn day?" Dino asked.

Saleem was allowed to slump to the ground, where he lay in a pool of his own blood.

Dino got behind the wheel of the car and waited until his partners had driven out of the alley and back onto the street. Then he turned on the radio and tuned in a local rock station. Gunning the engine, he sped out of the alley, enjoying the Chrysler's power.

TWENTY MINUTES LATER a cursing, handcuffed Dino was sitting in the rear of an LAPD patrol car. While one of the officers inspected the Chrysler, the other radioed in to the dispatcher that they had a suspected stolen car, and a driver who had been trying to outrun them who had fresh bloodstains on his clothing.

The LAPD, responding to a call from Washington, had details of the car in their computer system. Hal

Brognola, already in the city, was escorted to the police facility where the car would soon be taken.

Using a secure telephone line, the big Fed spoke to Barbara Price, asking her to inform Mack Bolan what had happened and to tell him that his trip to Los Angeles was top priority now.

15

"LAPD have dusted it for prints and sent the results to be checked through the central computer," Brognola said.

Mack Bolan circled the Chrysler, which was parked in a corner of the police impounding facility. The last time he had seen the car it had been parked outside the ski lodge in Colorado, and Gazli was having it loaded before he and his men drove away.

"Even if we come up with a match, I don't expect it to help us much," Bolan observed. "The only way we're going to get our hands on these terrorists is by direct action." He caught Brognola's eye. "Did you speak to the news team?"

Brognola grunted. "For as much good it did. They accept that their job puts them at risk, but they won't cancel anything. The guy in charge, Jerry Brookner, said he wasn't going to duck and run just because some terrorists make noise. He's a hardcase, Striker. Argues there's no point in going under cover. The way he sees it, if there's a threat to their lives, postponing it today isn't going to make it go away. We can shut them away now, but there's still tomorrow, and the next day. Next year. And we can't be around to protect them for the rest of their lives."

"The guy does have a point, Hal," Bolan admitted. "At least this time around we do know the terrorists are in the area. Next time the threat could come from anyone, anywhere."

"Yeah, yeah. I know. That's what makes it hard—knowing Brookner is right."

"And we still have Rachim Gazli and his crew running around loose."

"Your call, Striker. The mission brief still stands."

"Update me on what the LAPD have so far."

"Dino Marchetti is just a local small-time hood. His main business is stolen cars. The way he tells it, he was contracted to take the Chrysler and destroy it. Make sure there was nothing left to trace. But he got greedy and decided to sell it to a dealer and pocket the cash instead. His client didn't want that, so Dino killed him. The police have got him for that. Blood on his clothes, and he still had the knife in his pocket with the victim's blood on it.

"The victim turned out to be a young man named Saleem Pradesh. There's nothing on file about him. According to the police, he was clean."

Bolan had opened the car's rear door and checked the interior. He spotted the car phone and picked it up. After a moment's thought he punched in the number that would connect him with Stony Man, following its electronic rerouting. When his call was answered he asked to be put through to Aaron Kurtzman.

"Hey, big guy, you must need help if you're calling me," the Bear rumbled.

"Got a mobile phone here," Bolan said. He read off the phone's number. "Run this down and find out all the calls made from it during the past twenty-four hours.''

"Okay. Give me a couple of hours, and I'll have everything you'll ever need to know.''

"You got something, Striker?'' Brognola asked.

"A long shot. Maybe Gazli contacted his man in L.A. so they could meet up and exchange vehicles. He was coming in from a long way off with no guarantees he could make a rendezvous exactly on time without a final check in.''

Brognola walked alongside Bolan as they left the garage and returned to the car the big Fed was using. Jack Grimaldi stood beside the vehicle.

"Jack, I want you to stay with Hal,'' Bolan said. "This thing is coming pretty close. Tail those newspeople but keep your distance unless something breaks.''

"Where are you going?'' Grimaldi asked.

"To see if I can find out who Saleem Pradesh was running with. He's involved in this somehow.''

Bolan picked up the car Brognola had obtained for him from the local branch of the Justice Department. It was a new Ford, fitted with a mobile phone that would enable the Executioner to keep in touch with Brognola and also contact Stony Man for any Intel.

He pulled out into the late-afternoon traffic and picked up the signs for East L.A.

As he pushed through the traffic, Bolan saw dark clouds rolling in from the west. Within a half hour it began to rain. At first it was light, but by the time he reached the Harbor Freeway, it was falling heavily. He switched on the wipers, peering through the streaked windshield at the exit signs.

It was still raining as Bolan coasted along the street where the grocery store run by Saleem Pradesh's grandfather was situated.

Bolan pulled in at the curb and checked the street. He had parked outside a local diner. Its windows were steamed up, but the warrior could see light glowing inside the establishment. Across from where he sat he could see the grocery store. It was shrouded in darkness, the shutters closed, out of respect for the death of the young man.

The street itself was quiet, with only a few cars parked at the curbs. The rain-washed sidewalks were deserted.

Bolan secured the Beretta 93-R in its shoulder holster before zipping up the leather jacket he was wearing over a black roll-neck sweater. He climbed out of the car and locked the door, then crossed the sidewalk and entered the diner.

The aroma of hot coffee filled Bolan's nostrils. The diner had only a few customers, huddled over their drinks in the isolation of the booths that ran along the main wall. Bolan took one of the empty stools at the counter, ordering a coffee and a sandwich. The counterman poured Bolan a cup of the coffee before he called through the order.

"Bad night," Bolan said. "Quiet one, too," he added, glancing around the diner.

"It's early yet," the counterman replied. "The rain could keep some of my regulars indoors."

"Do they always close the stores around here when it rains?"

"Say what?"

"I noticed the grocery store across the street is closed. I'd hoped to pick up a few things."

"Yeah, well, they had a death in the family. One of the younger ones," the counterman explained, warming to the subject. He was glad to have someone to talk to, the evening being so quiet. "He got himself killed. Throat cut, so I hear."

"That bad?"

"Damn right."

"He get mugged or something?"

"Nah! Some fallout over a stolen car. That's what I heard."

Bolan pushed his empty cup across the counter. "That's some good coffee you have there. I'd appreciate some more. So this guy was in the stolen-car business, you say."

"No, it wasn't that way. This young guy—Saleem—he was as straight as they come. So everybody thought. Now they can't figure out what he was up to."

"Must be hard on his family and friends."

"I guess so. It's going to be hard on Jaffir. He's the closest thing the kid had to a father. Saleem lost his own back in Iran or Iraq somewhere. Jaffir kind of took him under his wing. The kid used to run errands for him. Used to spend a lot of time with him."

Bolan's sandwich arrived. A couple more customers came in, and the counterman drifted off. Finishing his meal, the warrior paid the tab and returned to his car. He picked up the mobile phone and contacted Kurtzman.

"Anything for me?"

"There were two calls from that mobile number you asked me to check," Kurtzman said, "both to L.A. I ran down the number. Got you an address and a name."

"Is there a Jaffir in there?"

Kurtzman grunted. "I suppose you've been doing some snooping on your own."

"Some," Bolan admitted. "What do we know about this guy?"

"Jaffir Khalil runs a company that services restaurants catering to Middle Eastern tastes. His kitchens prepare traditional dishes, supply decorations. He also runs an employment agency for Muslims."

"So he's used to moving people around, finding them places to stay. That's the kind of organization our terrorists could make good use of."

"My thoughts, Striker."

"Any deeper background information?"

"Nothing. Khalil is clean. My guess would have him down as a sleeper. They're the worst to find because they haven't done a damn thing up to the day they're activated. Until then they behave like model citizens, obey all the rules and stay out of trouble. There's nothing on file, so they can move about unnoticed. The way I read it, this could be our boy Jaffir."

"Maybe he's broken the rules this time," Bolan said.

"That makes him all yours, Striker. Watch your back. Don't expect anything but the worst if he turns out to be one of your terrorists."

Before Kurtzman broke the connection, he gave Bolan the location of Jaffir Khalil's company and his home address.

Starting the car, Bolan drove off into the L.A. night, sensing the uneasy calm that prevailed. This part of the city had its troubles, rooted in the past. Those roots had a firm hold, and they could only add up to a hard time for the Executioner. That did little to faze Mack Bolan. He had walked the line far too many times to allow himself the luxury of backsliding.

The Executioner was on a collision course, like a heat-seeking missile that had its target spotted and locked on for impact. Before the final strike, there would be move and countermove, each side attempting to outthink the other. Inevitably the clash would come, and with it, the shadow of Death, waiting for the smoke to clear so it could claim its prize.

RAIN BOUNCED OFF the road and hammered against the roof of Bolan's Ford as he studied the building that housed Jaffir Khalil's company.

It was situated along a commercial strip, surrounded by dark, silent buildings shut down for the night. The Khalil building was the only one still showing signs of activity. Bolan had identified a couple of figures patrolling the property, and a light showed in one of the upper windows.

Outwardly there was nothing to indicate anything illegal going on. The patrolling figures could have been security guards and the lighted window an indication of someone working late in an office.

But it was worth a look.

The warrior unzipped the carryall on the seat beside him and took out a couple of spare magazines for the Beretta 93-R, which he pocketed. He also chose a thin garrote. He hesitated over the Desert Eagle, then decided against taking it. The massive handgun was difficult to conceal when he wore street clothing.

Armed and ready, Bolan eased out of the car, locking it before melting into the shadows. He slipped from one block of darkness to another, silent and unobtrusive in the gloom.

He approached the company building from the side. There were no security fences around any of the structures, so all Bolan had to do was step over the low wall separating the buildings. He remained in the shadows until the first of the roving guards came into sight. Watching the man, the warrior saw him pause to adjust the hang of a stubby MAC-10 subgun slung from one shoulder, then pull his jacket over it.

Instinct made the Executioner look over his shoulder. Framed in the rain-hazed light from a security light high on the wall, the other guard stood at the building's rear corner. He was a blurred, dark form, and Bolan couldn't tell whether he had a weapon in his hands. The guy seemed to be looking directly at him. After what seemed an eternity, the man advanced toward Bolan.

The warrior checked out the first guard. He had his body turned away, shoulders hunched against the falling rain, head tilted forward to keep it out of his eyes. He moved slowly, stepping out of Bolan's range of vision around the front of the building. From the way both men were acting, it appeared they were unaware of each other's immediate presence.

Now Bolan could hear the second guard. His footsteps were light but audible.

Hugging the wall of the building, Bolan blessed the night and the falling rain. The lack of any close light source also meant that this area of the building was in shadow. He hoped it was enough to conceal his presence.

The advancing guard was muttering to himself, no doubt complaining at having to spend his evening out in such inclement weather. He closed in on the spot where Bolan was waiting. The guy's coat flapped open and revealed the square outline of a shoulder-hung Ingram MAC-10. He clamped a hand to the offending garment and dragged it back to cover the weapon.

And then he stopped dead in his tracks, on a level with Bolan's motionless form. Even in the pale light, the warrior made out the gleam in the guy's eye. The hand that had moments before covered the Ingram now sought to expose it.

Bolan's left fist punched the guard in the side of the head, just above the right eye. The stunning impact snapped the man's head around in a whiplash sweep, turning him bodily away from Bolan as the Executioner eased out from the wall to complete his attack.

There was no time for a fancy maneuver. The warrior kicked the guard at the back of one knee, causing him to stumble. As he leaned backward to regain his balance, Bolan coiled his arms around the guy's neck, closing the loop of flesh to cut off air and the flow of blood. The guard began to struggle, aware of his approaching demise. Bolan leaned back, straightening his legs to lift the guy off his feet and put more pressure on his stranglehold. Clawing hands reached up to try to dislodge the warrior's grip. The effort was too little too late. Bolan increased the pressure and heard a desperate gurgle come from the guard's throat, felt the panicked thrash of feet attempting to find solid ground. The guy's body shuddered, twisted back and forth. He arched his spine, and with a final spasm the struggles ceased. Bolan held on for long seconds before he lowered the corpse to the ground, pushing it against the base of the wall.

Moving quickly along the side of the building, the warrior rounded the far end and found himself near the loading bays. He took the short flight of steps two at a time and stood under the cover of the roofed loading area. Wiping the rain from his face, he catfooted across the wooden platform until he was confronted by the row of roller doors that allowed access to the warehouse section of the building. They were closed, but he located a small access door in the wall. It was old, as was the building, and constructed of wood.

He took a step back, raised his foot and drove it against the lock plate. The door splintered and crashed back against the inner wall.

Bolan crossed the threshold, ducking low and stepping to one side of the door as he scanned the interior of the building. He took quick note of the boxes and barrels, the stacks of foodstuffs on metal racks.

His entrance had attracted attention.

Voices broke the silence from above his head. Bolan crouched beside a stack of cartons and located the source of the voices. They came from a walkway on the upper level, where offices overlooked the main warehouse area. A couple of low-wattage lights glowed up there, enabling Bolan to make out the figures of two men who emerged from one of the offices. They were conversing rapidly to each other in Farsi. More importantly, Bolan caught the gleam of light on the dull metal of gun barrels.

One man paused, leaning over the railing that edged the walkway, and apparently instructed his partner to check the warehouse. His words were accompanied by arm waving while he scanned the warehouse.

The man coming down the stairs held his pistol in a two-handed grip, the muzzle darting back and forth as he searched the shadows. His stance was correct, and he studied each point his weapon covered before moving to the next.

His precautions were in vain.

They did nothing to save him from the 9 mm parabellum rounds that winged from the muzzle of Bolan's suppressed 93-R. The triburst planted three slugs in the gunner's chest, knocking him back against the stair railing. He lay there for a few seconds, then slid down to the bottom.

Before the dead man stopped moving, Bolan had changed position. Careful as he was, the man up on the walkway picked up his shadow. He turned instantly, opening fire and laying down a trail of slugs that ripped into boxes and chewed open sacks of flour.

Bolan slid on his knees, bracing his gun hand across the top of a carton. He aimed and fired almost in one breath. The Beretta chugged out three rounds, and the gunner on the walkway flipped backward. He tumbled through an open door and crashed to the floor. His heels drummed against the floor, protesting the advance of death, and by the time Bolan had sprinted up the stairs, the guy had lost his struggle and was already in eternity.

The Executioner peered into the office the two men had exited. A number of opened boxes sat on a table and the chairs that stood around the room. The boxes contained Kalashnikov AK-74s, brand-new and still wrapped in protective paper. There were also a number of ammunition boxes, holding filled magazines of 5.45 mm bullets.

If these were what Khalil's clients were ordering through his company, he had a strange idea about what a service company was.

Bolan heard the distant sound of a closing door. He left the office and moved along the walkway until he reached an unlit spot. Crouching, he peered through the railings and scanned the warehouse floor.

The first guard he had spotted outside, alerted by the shooting, had come to check. He called out for his companions, and when he received no reply he began to curse. Bolan didn't need to understand the language. He knew swearing when he heard it.

The gunner leveled his Ingram as he approached the stairs and saw the dead man. He started up the stairs, the MAC-10 tracking ahead of him.

Bolan rose to his full height, the Beretta angling down to a spot just above the top step. He held the autopistol two-handed. The guard's dark hair bobbed into view, followed by the exposed flesh of his forehead.

The 93-R chugged its deadly greeting. The triburst cored the terrorist's skull, blowing out the rear in a glutinous red mass. The Disciple of Khalfi arched backward, his writhing form falling in a slow curve until he struck the stairs near the bottom.

The warrior returned to the office and the weapons cache. Inside one of the open crates he found a sheaf of papers lying on top of the weapons. The individual sheets held names, locations and numbers, and the Executioner realized he was holding a distribution list. Jaffir Khalil was distributing more than ethnic food. The company vehicles were probably used to deliver the weapons. Going about their everyday business, they would be unlikely to arouse much suspicion.

Bolan made a quick search of the other offices, but found little of interest, apart from a telephone and fax machine.

"Striker," he said when his call to Stony Man was answered.

"We'll have to stop meeting this way," Barbara Price said. "Do we have a problem?"

"I'm at Khalil's company. I ran into some night workers, only they weren't packing food. They have a sideline—brand-new AK-74s. A sizable consignment, too."

"Hold on, Striker, the boss man is on the other line. I'll patch him through."

Brognola's acknowledgment came through moments later. He listened in silence to Bolan's information.

"Suggestions?"

"Arrange a pickup of the weapons fast," Bolan stated, "then put the place under surveillance in case someone turns up looking for them."

"Will do," Brognola agreed. "I want those things locked away. You find anything useful?"

"Yeah. Looks like a distribution list. Names and locations all around the Southern California area, with how many guns to go to each one. Barbara, stand by, I'm going to fax the lists through to you."

Bolan fed the sheets into the fax machine and keyed in the secure number that would transmit the list through to Stony Man. While the sheets went through, the Executioner resumed the conversation.

"This group is better established than we figured."

"Anything on Gazli's whereabouts?"

"Nothing," Bolan admitted. "The weapons are a bonus I wasn't expecting. But I need a line on the terrorist. Whatever he's planning is going to happen soon. My gut feeling tells me we're running out of time."

"A change in the game plan?"

"To what? Hal, we've got Brookner and his people covered. All we can do is go with the flow. The situation's difficult. We can't pinpoint Gazli because we don't have enough information. He's going to lie low right up to the time of the hit. If he does get his people through to Brookner and company, we could have a massacre on our hands. Gazli won't surrender even if he's cornered. He'd set off those explosive devices and take as many people with him as he could. We're in a no-win situation here. Right now Gazli is making the rules. He'll choose the time and the place. It's his call—unless I can get to him first."

"Striker, it's down to you. You can recognize him. No one else can. What's your next move?"

"Khalil," Bolan replied. "He's the only link, the only connection between me and Gazli. I have to find him, and I have to break him."

16

A fine mist drifting in off the Pacific hung over the Malibu area. Bolan's watch read 6:30 a.m. He had parked the Ford off the highway, then crossed to work his way down the crumbling headland until he reached the beach.

Crouching in the sand, hidden from view by tumbled rock close to the base of the slope, the warrior studied the hazy outline of the beach house owned by Jaffir Khalil.

Information sent to Brognola from Kurtzman had been waiting when the Executioner joined the big Fed at the LAPD office. Bolan, taking time for a mug of hot coffee and sandwiches courtesy of the police department, had scanned the information on the man.

Bolan wasn't particularly interested in the standard details about Khalil. According to the file, the man was a hard-working citizen who had built up his company from small beginnings. As well as the distribution company, Khalil had a good record in the property market. He seemed to have the knack of buying cheap and selling high. His instinct for a good deal had netted him a considerable bank balance. Politically Khalil was dormant. He kept his own counsel where politics and religion were concerned, staying well within the law and avoiding conflict. Until now. Despite the outward impressions he gave, Khalil was deeply involved in the Disciples of Khalfi mission to America.

There had even been a passport photograph of Khalil included in the documentation. Bolan had studied the man's face, trying to look beyond the fixed stare, which gave nothing away.

The personal information had provided Bolan with the location of Khalil's home, a beachside house in Malibu. The Executioner felt certain that Rachim Gazli wouldn't be resident there. The terrorist would be housed somewhere else in the L.A. area.

His only course of action was to locate Khalil and persuade the man to part with that vital piece of information.

Clad in a blacksuit and fully armed, Bolan hunkered in the damp sand and planned his assault on Khalil's home.

It had been constructed on a rocky headland, as had many of the houses in the area that looked out over the beach. Stone steps offered access to the house from the beach. Bolan could make out a roofed porch running the length of the house's rear. Thick shrubbery bounded the sides of the house, as did similar growths at the front, facing the highway.

Satisfied that there were no outside guards, Bolan made his way along the base of the slope until he was directly beneath the house. He dismissed the steps. If he used them, he would be in full view of anyone in the house.

Choosing his spot, Bolan began to climb the outcrop that supported the house. He moved slowly, taking his time over each foot- and handhold. The rock seemed to be solid, but there was nothing to be gained by dislodging loose sections. Other than a risk to himself in a fall, there was the added possibility of alerting anyone in the house.

It took the warrior almost fifteen minutes to scale the outcrop. He finally made it to a narrow curve of rock that offered temporary refuge while he regained his breath.

He had been squatting underneath the wooden porch floor. When he had rested, Bolan leaned out and gripped the lower edge of the porch and pulled himself upright until he was able to peer between the slats of the porch railing. The house lay still and silent, with only the gentle sway of a potted plant suspended from one of the cross beams disturbing the stillness.

The warrior quickly hauled himself up and over the railing, moving along the porch until he reached the rear door. He turned the knob and found it was locked. Bolan removed a lock pick from a slit pocket of the blacksuit and went to work. The house had not yet been fitted with modern locks, and the one he worked on yielded after a minute of careful manipulation. Bolan put away the pick and unholstered the suppressed Beretta, switching the selector to single-shot mode.

Turning the doorknob slowly, Bolan cracked the door. He refrained from opening it fully until he had checked the frame for an alarm. There didn't seem to be one, so he pushed the door open just wide enough for him to slip through. Once inside, he pulled the door shut behind him.

He stood motionless in the kitchen, his ears attuned for any sound that might disturb the calm.

Nothing.

The warrior waited an additional few minutes before catfooting across the floor and pausing at the open door on the other side of the room.

The kitchen opened onto the expansive living area. It was an open-plan, low-ceilinged affair with furniture scattered in a loose arrangement. Rugs lay on the polished wood floor. The walls were hung with paintings. To Bolan's left, the living room extended out over the porch area, with large windows giving unrestricted views of the beach area and the ocean.

Doors led off to other parts of the house from the living room. Bolan crossed to check them out.

He was halfway across the room when he caught a soft sound. Turning in the direction of the disturbance, Bolan spotted movement. A large black leather couch, with its backrest toward the warrior, stood in the center of the room. A heavyset man with thick hair and beard sat up abruptly, head and shoulders rising above the couch. The gleaming shape of a chrome-steel autopistol followed, the muzzle turning in Bolan's direction.

Survival instincts took command, ordering a rapid response. Bolan took a headlong dive to the floor, skidding across the smooth, waxed surface.

He heard the solid clap of sound from the autopistol, the powerful slug gouging a ragged furrow across the floor.

The Executioner came to rest against a wall and turned on his side, the Beretta angled at the bearded man's position. The man's wide bulk rose up off the couch. He was naked to the waist, his upper body covered with black hair. His huge hands were turning the autopistol at Bolan, his finger pulling back on the trigger.

The 93-R coughed once, then again. The 9 mm slugs burned into the big guy's barrel chest, cleaving flesh and muscle, chewing their way to his pumping heart. He gave a surprised grunt as the parabellum rounds did their work, the rapid onslaught of bodily shock paralyzing him for long seconds. Internally he was near death already, his ruptured heart reducing the circulation of blood around his massive frame. He toppled forward, over the couch's backrest, and crashed to the floor. The bulk of his prone body began to spasm. Fingers of blood leaked out from under him, creeping across the floorboards.

Bolan pushed to his feet, already moving on. His mind was alert for further threats as he eased through the open archway that led to the far side of the house.

A crash of sound brought his senses to full awareness. The noise came from a door on his immediate right, and it was followed by the unmistakable sound of a man cursing.

Bolan reached the door and hit it with his shoulder, then stepped to one side as it swung open. Gunfire erupted from inside the room, the bullets thudding into the wall opposite. Plaster blew out and a framed picture crashed to the floor.

Crouching low, powered by the knowledge of time slipping away, the warrior went into the room on the crack of the final shot. He executed a shoulder roll, sending a chair skittering across the floor. Flat on his stomach, the Beretta ahead of him, Bolan picked up on the lean outline of a man clad in dark pajamas darting for the door. Even in that split second he recognized the face of Jaffir Khalil.

The Executioner pushed to one knee, reaching out to grab the leg of the chair he'd collided with and thrust it across Khalil's path. Man and chair became tangled. Khalil's anger and pain were expressed in a single yell as he tripped and sprawled his length across the floor, the gun in his right hand jarred loose.

Straightening, Bolan took two long strides and towered above his adversary, the Beretta pointed at the man's head.

"No!" Khalil screamed, the one word expressing his anger and his contempt for Bolan and everything he stood for.

With a surprising turn of speed he swept his right leg around, knocking Bolan's feet from under him. The Stony Man warrior was slammed to the floor, his shoulders taking the main impact, but there was enough force left to render him momentarily at a disadvantage.

Khalil lunged at him, his clawing fingers reaching for Bolan's throat. They closed with ferocious strength, starting to shut off the warrior's wind.

Bolan swept up the Beretta, slamming it against Khalil's temple. The blow opened a gash that began to bleed immediately. Khalil snarled, lips peeling back from clenched teeth. His eyes widened with the burst of pain following the blow, but he maintained his grip. Bolan lashed out again, landing a second blow directly over the first. This time the pressure of Khalil's fingers slackened. The warrior utilized the moment to twist his prone body and dislodge his adversary. He slid his free arm under Khalil's and levered him aside. The terrorist rolled, springing to his feet and returning to the attack as Bolan himself came upright. He ignored the threat of the Beretta, as if aware that Bolan wasn't going to kill him. He knew the warrior needed him for information, and that fact gave him a certain advantage.

Khalil, already close, slammed into Bolan, throwing his arms around the big man. The pair teetered for a moment, then staggered off balance. The back of Bolan's legs caught against the edge of the room's bed, and he went down. Khalil made a wild grab for Bolan's gun arm, caught it and clamped both hands around it, levering back.

Steeling himself against the pain, Bolan drove the heel of his left hand into Khalil's side, over the ribs. He repeated the blow, putting everything into the assault. A ragged moan bubbled from Khalil's lips as the effect of Bolan's blows registered. His lean torso arched upward, giving the warrior the opportunity to club him across the jaw. The solid punch snapped Khalil's head to one side. Blood trickled from a corner of his mouth.

Bolan lodged his palm under Khalil's chin and pushed upward, stretching the terrorist's neck until bones grated. As Khalil's body lifted away from him, the warrior doubled his right leg under him, levering Khalil upright. The moment Bolan was able to wedge his foot against Khalil's stomach, he straightened his leg, putting every ounce of strength he could into the thrust. Khalil was catapulted across the room, arms windmilling, body twisting as he tried to control himself. He slammed into the wall, the back of his skull thudding against it.

Turning, Bolan spotted Khalil's pistol. He picked up the weapon and slid it under his belt.

Crossing the room, Bolan grabbed Khalil's collar and hauled the man to his feet. He dragged the terrorist out of the room and through the archway into the living room. Khalil, feet trying to gain contact with the floor, failed to dredge up any reserves of strength. The Executioner pushed him into a leather armchair, then bent to retrieve the dead bodyguard's pistol. He dropped out the magazine and tossed the pistol across the room. Then he holstered the 93-R and unleathered the massive Desert Eagle. Returning to where Khalil sprawled in the armchair, Bolan touched the muzzle of the pistol against the terrorist's forehead.

"We need to talk."

Khalil stared up at the grim face of the Executioner and recognized Death in human form.

"There is nothing we have to say to each other, American."

"Your choice," Bolan replied. "Makes no difference to me. But your days are numbered. And freedom ends here and now, Khalil. Make no mistake. Today is the last day you'll ever wake up in your own bed. For the rest of your life your world will be no larger than a prison cell."

Khalil studied Bolan's face, and he was able to read the chill message in the American's eyes. He was no longer a free man, able to come and go whenever and wherever he wanted. The prospect wasn't pleasing.

"Your words do not frighten me," he said, desperate to maintain an honorable front. "If I am to become a prisoner, then so be it. I have my rights. They will protect me."

"Rights? Remind me, Khalil."

The terrorist wiped blood from his chin. "As a prisoner of war I am entitled to be treated with respect. You cannot torture me and I must be dealt with fairly."

Bolan stepped back, a faintly mocking smile touching the edges of his mouth.

"We need to correct a few things here. You are not a prisoner of war, Khalil. There's been no formal declaration of war between our two countries. You and your group have been involved in illegal acts of terrorism. So don't come on with the old excuse of whining about your rights. What about the rights of the people dead through your acts? Did anyone ask them how they felt?"

"There will always be casualties," Khalil stated. "How many of my brothers have you killed?"

"Only those who deserved to die through their actions, the ones who came to this country with the sole intention of killing Americans. Don't think that wrapping up your crimes in religious cant makes them anything more than just crimes. Air your grievances like men. Not back-street dogs crawling in the gutter."

"You are wrong!" Khalil yelled. "The Disciples of Khalfi are brothers of Islam! We fight for our cause against the American heretics who wish only to grind us beneath their heels."

Bolan noted the rise in pitch of Khalil's voice. The shrillness should have warned him, but awareness came a fraction of a second too late.

Khalil lunged up out of the armchair, one hand slashing out to push the muzzle of the Desert Eagle away from his head. Bolan's finger jerked back on the trigger and the powerful gun discharged, the heavy bullet thudding into the wall on the far side of the room. By this time Khalil's momentum had carried him forward into Bolan. As the Executioner attempted to regain his balance, he felt Khalil's fingers free the handgun tucked behind his belt.

Khalil's bloody face wore an expression of triumph as he began to pull the pistol on line for a shot.

His move was paralleled by Bolan's own response. As the warrior fell, he clamped the big .44 Magnum pistol in both fists, tracked the muzzle on Khalil's lean form and pulled the trigger.

The noise of the single shot from Khalil's weapon was lost in the two big booms from the Executioner's massive weapon. The large-caliber slugs chewed into Khalil's chest, silencing forever the terrorist's bigoted rhetoric. Khalil was driven back by the impact of the slugs, his stricken form impacting against the panoramic window overlooking the beach. The glass shattered, and the man was dumped on the porch amid glittering shards.

Bolan gained his feet, aware of a sting of pain across his left upper arm, where Khalil's bullet had left a ragged tear. He moved to the window, looking down at Khalil's bloody corpse.

The Disciple of Khalfi lay on his back, his sightless eyes staring out of a blood-streaked face.

Bolan had come out on top from his confrontation with the fanatical terrorist, but the termination of Khalil's life had also removed any chance he might have had to gain information from the man.

17

Hal Brognola stood beside Bolan and watched the body being removed from the porch.

"Damn bad luck, Striker," he said.

The warrior shrugged. "The way he felt, I don't think he would have told me anything."

Brognola shoved his topcoat open and thrust his hands deep in the pockets of his trousers. He gazed around the living room of the beach house.

"Maybe we can pick something up here," he said hopefully.

Bolan had already moved across the room to check out a desk that stood in one corner. He flexed his left arm as he moved, conscious of the dressing one of the medics had placed there after dealing with the bullet wound.

Since contacting Brognola, the warrior had searched the house. All he'd come up with were some secreted weapons and ammunition. There was some anti-American literature, as well, hidden in a waterproof wrapper in the toilet tank.

He hadn't found any strong connection with Rachim Gazli and his plans. He accepted that there might not be anything written down. The assassination strike might simply have been carried around inside the heads of those involved.

When Brognola and his team had arrived, Bolan stood aside while they carried out their routine work—removal of the bodies and the weapons used. The house had been checked again in case there were more weapons, and the warrior reluctantly took the time to have his wound cleaned and stitched by a medic.

Now he was chafing to be operational again, strongly aware of the relentless advance of time.

Sitting at the desk, Bolan went through each drawer, dumping the contents on the desk top. Brognola joined him, and they sifted through the collection of personal and business items. They found little to help them. Khalil had maintained detailed information on his legitimate business, but his terrorist activities were less than evident.

Bolan came across a manila folder and placed it on the desk. He opened it and went through the papers it contained. They were property deeds. According to the details, Khalil had been renting a beachfront house in Venice. He had negotiated the tenancy agreement a month ago, and it was for a period of six months, with an option for longer, if necessary.

"Why does he need another beach house when he has this one?" Brognola asked.

"I've got a pretty good idea," Bolan replied, writing down the address of the house.

"Give me a ride to my car," he said to Brognola. "I need to change before I go to Venice."

MIDMORNING WAS WARM and bright. Sunlight shimmered off the Pacific beyond crowded Venice Beach. On the street that paralleled the beach, open-fronted restaurants and shops that catered to all tastes vied for trade with street vendors and roving performers. The crowds of visitors had to share the space with the resident roller skaters and cyclists. The small beach town still maintained its innocent charm, the draw that had long been its main attraction.

Mack Bolan, moving along the busy walkway, regretted his inability to enjoy Venice's slightly faded appeal. He stood alone among the sightseers, a tall figure slightly apart from the crowd. Watching the faces of the passersby, the Executioner envied their freedom of choice, the innocent pleasure of their casual day. His envy, though, wasn't tinged with jealousy. His everlasting war, a self-imposed dedication to duty, denied him life's simple distractions. That denial was his choice alone. It was a confirmation of his fight against evil to see his fellow citizens able to live their lives as they should, without fear of oppression and violence.

The warrior could understand Khalil's decision to use Venice for his purpose. The beach town was used to people coming and going. Its existence was based on attracting visitors, so new faces in the area weren't unusual. Rachim Gazli and his men, appropriately dressed, would be seen as nothing more than tourists. As long as they maintained a low profile, no one would see any threat in their presence. They would be able to stay under cover until the day of the strike. Then the assassination team would leave as quietly as they had arrived, with no one any wiser.

Bolan reached the intersection he was searching for and stood counting off the houses. The one he wanted stood halfway along the row, a reasonably maintained frame house, painted in a powder-blue-and-white color scheme, with a short driveway at the side leading to an open carport.

Turning into the street, the warrior skirted the house, ducking into the alley that bounded the property. He loosened his light sport coat so that the Beretta was accessible. A weathered fence ran the length of the property. Midway along the alley Bolan passed a gate. He paused, trying the handle. The gate opened, and the warrior slipped through, closing the gate behind him. Pulling the Beretta from its shoulder rig, he hesitated beside a wheeled trash can, using it as cover while he scanned the area. The rear of the house had a paved patio area, surrounded by a fence. A barbecue and plastic furniture stood abandoned in the sunlight.

Checking out the house itself, Bolan was immediately struck by the prevailing silence. If people were inside, they were being too quiet. Gazli would have kept up the normal activities and accompanying noises had he still been there. The warrior knew before he reached the rear door that the terrorists had already gone.

The porch door gave under Bolan's hand, opening silently. He edged into the small, neat kitchen. Cooking odors lingered in the still, warm air, and sunshine penetrated the drawn slats of the window blind, tracing alternate strips of light and shadow across the room. On the table were recently used plates and cups. Bread crumbs on the plates were soft and moist. Moving to the stove, Bolan touched the coffeepot resting there. It was still warm to the touch.

He crossed the kitchen and walked to the front of the house, quickly checking the living room and bathroom. They both yielded evidence of having been recently vacated. Down the short hall, Bolan was confronted by two final doors. The bedrooms.

The first contained two single beds, the covers thrown back from use, the sheets showing where someone had lain.

The other bedroom held two more single beds. On one of them lay the trussed-up and naked body of a man. His wrists and ankles had been bound with thin wire, pulled so tight that the wire had been lost in the flesh swollen around it. A wide strip of adhesive tape covered the man's mouth. The corpse lay on what had originally been a white sheet. Now it was dark with the dried blood that had pulsed from the numerous knife slashes marking the body. The throat had also been cut, deeply and from ear to ear.

Bolan checked the body. It was cold and stiff, indicating that the man had been dead for a considerable amount of time.

Searching the house, the warrior found the telephone. He needed Brognola's clout to have the dead man identified as quickly as possible. There was a tie-in somewhere, and Bolan felt sure it had to do with the assassination attempt. Identifying the man might give Bolan the lead that would take him to Gazli and his team.

"HIS NAME WAS George Calder. Forty-three years old, divorced, lived in Anaheim, owned a catering business that provided for conventions and hotels in the Anaheim area. It's a medium business with a small work force, but had a high reputation."

"Did anyone report him missing?" Bolan asked.

The LAPD detective shook his head.

"We checked with his company. They said he was visiting with friends in Malibu. Due back today because the company has a catering contract to handle tonight."

"Where?"

"The Langton Towers Hotel in Anaheim. It's one of the new luxury hotels on Convention Way, near the Anaheim Convention Center."

"Thanks for your help, Lieutenant Adams," Brognola said. "I'm grateful for everything your people have done today. I'm sorry I can't be more open about this, but I'll explain at a better time."

Adams smiled. "I'll have to live with that for now. We'll keep this all under wraps, as requested. Don't keep me waiting too long. I need answers to a number of incidents we've had lately that haven't been explained."

He looked at Bolan as he spoke, something in his expression telling the Executioner that he understood the need for security, but he was mad as hell because he was being kept in the dark. Adams's penetrating stare also said he knew that Bolan was involved all the way down the line, and he was more than curious about this tall, taciturn man who asked pertinent questions without offense, yet commanded respect from everyone he came into contact with. Adams had also made a mental note of the still-visible marks on Bolan's face, marks that spoke of recent violence. He understood that this "Blanski" was some kind of government specialist, yet something more. The man carried himself lightly, giving an impression of casual ease, yet beneath that veneer there was a caged tiger just waiting to spring. Adams wished he could know more about the man.

Brognola followed Bolan out of the house. They walked back through Venice until they reached the warrior's parked Ford.

"That cop is so curious he won't sleep tonight," Brognola said, staring out to sea.

"You can't blame the way he feels."

"I know that, Striker, but we agree we can't broadcast too much about this terrorist group in case it pushes them over the edge before we locate them."

"I think we have located them, Hal. There must be something planned tonight at the Langton Towers, something that's going to involve Brookner and his team. Gazli knows they're going to be there. That's why Calder is dead. They need his company influence to get them into the hotel so they'll be there when Brookner and his people arrive."

"No need to ask where you're going."

Bolan unlocked his car and slid behind the wheel.

"I'll stay in touch. Tell Jack to stay close to Brookner. And see if you can scare up any more information about tonight."

Brognola raised a hand in farewell as Bolan drove away. As he turned he saw Lieutenant Adams approaching. The curious cop was just another one of the things the big Fed had to deal with. He sighed wearily. Sometimes he envied Bolan. The Executioner's world was one where problems were solved on a practical level. Brognola had to swim in the pool labeled protocol and compromise. His weapons were words and social niceties. And sometimes they were a real pain in the ass.

18

It was 2:15 p.m. when Rachim Gazli coasted the catering truck to a stop at the down-ramp entrance to the Langton Towers underground parking lot. He sat calmly waiting as the security man stepped out of his booth and approached.

"Calder Catering," Gazli stated. He pulled a sheet of paper from his work-shirt pocket and handed it to the uniformed man. "Got some fancy buffet to set up in the Skylight Lounge. Media party tonight. Some people have all the luck. Me, I have to get my own meals since the old lady upped and ran out."

The security man ran his eyes over the paper. It looked in order.

"I'd choose to make my own meals if mine would take a hike," he said, grinning at Gazli. He wrote out passes for the terrorist and his three assistants, then passed them through the window of the truck.

"If there's anything left over, I'll bag some up for you," Gazli promised. "Usually these people leave more than they eat. We take it away and it gets dumped in the trash."

The security man raised a hand. "Okay, then, don't forget me."

"I won't." Gazli slipped the truck into gear and waited for the guard to raise the barrier.

The truck rolled down the ramp and entered the parking area. Gazli drove to a far corner, reversing the vehicle until it was close to the concrete wall. He switched off the engine and sat in the silence, listening to the metal parts pinging as they began to cool. Finally he turned to his three companions.

"Remember to speak English at all times. Don't give anyone any cause to doubt us. Be polite. Until the time to strike, we are employees of Calder Catering. We set up the buffet as Jaffir explained to us. Nothing else. And then we wait."

The rear of the truck opened to show the carts that held all the prepared food. Under Gazli's instruction, they were wheeled out of the truck.

"Yamir, you will stay with the truck."

The young terrorist nodded in understanding. In their aluminum cases, stored in a locker inside the vehicle, were the explosive devices they would use to destroy the news team.

"No one will get to them," he stated.

Gazli and his companions changed into the white coats and trousers stored in the cab of the truck, then donned white peaked caps. Each man carried a compact Beretta Model 84, supplied by Khalil. The pocket-sized weapons had a magazine capacity of thirteen rounds and were easily concealed under their coats.

Pushing the first of the food carts, Gazli led the way to the service elevator that would take them to the Skylight Lounge. The doors opened at the touch of the button, and the three men stepped inside.

As the elevator began to ascend, Gazli smiled in grim satisfaction. Finally events were going their way. This, the most important part of their mission, was coming to fruition.

The execution of the plan had been almost childishly simple.

Jaffir Khalil, through his connections within the local catering industry, had learned about a surprise celebration for the man named Brookner and his film crew. The media company they worked for had an award to present to the news team, recognition for their recent journalistic reports. The news had come while Khalil had been gathering information on the movements of the news team while it was in the Los Angeles area, and had been a stroke of luck none of them could have anticipated. If they were able to utilize the knowledge to their advantage, the Disciples would be able to carry out their predetermined execution and create the maximum result. Not only would Brookner and his crew die as ordained, the additional deaths and resultant damage to the prestigious hotel would gain massive publicity. The affair would highlight the vulnerability of the Americans, even in their luxurious palaces of pleasure.

With the time and location of the celebration fixed, all Gazli needed was a way in. Once again the resourceful Khalil was able to provide for them.

He had found out that the company responsible for providing the catering was the one owned by George Calder, whom he knew through business, and it was an easy matter to arrange a meeting with the man on the pretext of discussing further business. Since the departure of his wayward wife, Calder had thrown himself into running his business. It was the only thing he cared about. He lived for his business.

He died because of it.

Khalil arranged to meet Calder at the Malibu beach house. Once inside, Calder became a hostage in a game he failed to comprehend. From Malibu he was taken to Venice, to the rented house he would never leave alive. Stripped and bound, Calder was terrorized into revealing the details of the contract he had with the Langton Towers.

His subsequent death was simply a gesture of the contempt felt by Gazli and his brothers for the people they had come to terrorize, a grim warning that the Disciples of Khalfi were able to walk the streets of America with impunity.

Gazli left the house in Venice armed with the knowledge of the delivery truck's route and timetable. With the plan fixed firmly in his head, he deployed his group. They were able to stop the truck as it entered an underpass by the simple expedient of faking a breakdown that caused the truck to make an emergency stop. The truck driver, ready to bawl out the car driver, lost his voice when Gazli climbed into the rear of the double cab and put a gun to the back of his head. The choice for the driver was simple. Drive on—or die. He made his decision and the truck emerged from the underpass moments later, with Gazli's car falling in behind.

A diversion, mapped out by Khalil, was made. They turned onto a quiet street off the main drag, which was followed by a brief stop at the rear of an empty building. The truck driver and his partner were both shot, the suppressed discharges attracting no attention. The bodies were placed in the trunk of Gazli's car, which was abandoned in a multistory parking lot on the drive in to Anaheim.

With the terrorist leader behind the wheel, the catering truck resumed its journey to Anaheim.

THE FOOD CARTS made no sound as they rolled along the plush carpeting of the corridor leading to the Skylight Lounge.

Gazli felt strangely calm and optimistic. Something told him everything would be all right. The disappointments of the past few days, due mainly to the interference of the American warrior, were behind them. The up side was that despite the aggravation, the plan was still on course. His nemesis might have delayed matters and caused distractions, but Gazli and his brothers were still active, and making their final preparations right under the noses of the Americans.

They reached the double doors to the suite and pushed the carts inside. At the top end of the spacious room, with its dark blue ceiling decorated with glittering pinpoints of silver light, long tables covered with white tablecloths waited for the food Gazli and his men were delivering.

"We must have everything ready by five," the terrorist leader stated. "Go and bring the other carts."

Left on his own, Gazli began to place the prepared dishes on the table. The task was depressing but necessary. He carried out the operation without thought, his mind on other matters.

The success of the mission could be achieved only by the sacrifices of Salim and Abrim, the brothers who were collecting the remaining carts. They would wear the explosive devices that would destroy Brookner and his people. The powerful, contained detonations would be strong enough to kill everyone within the confines of the Skylight Lounge. Gazli regretted the imminent deaths of his brothers. Their commitment to the cause was absolute, as was his own. They had volunteered to carry the bombs, sincere in their belief that what they were going to do would be a significant victory for the Disciples of Khalfi and Islam. Whatever followed would be generated by the impact of the current mission and would strengthen the cause of the holy war.

Gazli paused, surveying the rich spread of food he was laying out across the table. It was food enough to feed several starving families for a week. The Americans were so rich in material things that they wasted it wholesale. The invited guests would pick and nibble at the food, leaving much of it untouched. The thought angered Gazli, and he was forced to mentally step back and calm himself. This was not the time or place to allow his emotions to distract him from his course. Breathing deeply, the terrorist leader turned back to the cart he was unloading and continued to place the dishes on the table.

Salim and Abrim returned with the last of the food carts. They worked alongside their leader, laying out the food, paper plates and napkins. Plastic utensils were placed at the end of each table for the guests to help themselves.

With less than an hour to go before the guests would begin to arrive, Gazli gestured to his brothers. They withdrew to make their way back down to the truck, taking one of the empty carts with them.

Behind the truck, the three Disciples changed into the black trousers and white shirts with black ties that Khalil had obtained for them. White jackets went over the uniforms.

Yamir transferred the aluminum cases that contained the explosive devices into the cart, as well as three fully loaded Ingrams with spare magazines.

They checked their watches.

"The guests begin to arrive at five. Brookner and his crew will come in some time later. Once they are in the lounge, we will go ahead. The longer we wait, the more the chances of being discovered."

There was a moment of farewell as Salim and Abrim embraced Yamir. He knew he wouldn't see them again.

"Go with God, my brothers. What you achieve today will be long remembered."

Salim and Abrim returned to the elevator, pushing the loaded cart between them.

"Wait until five-thirty," Gazli instructed Yamir. "Go to the public parking area by the walkway over there. The car Jaffir arranged will be parked beside the stairwell. Here is the key. It is a gray Oldsmobile with a rear-window sticker saying, "Buy U.S. for the Best." If I have not joined you within five minutes, leave. Do not try to find me. Make your way out of the city and return to Colorado. I will join you if I can. If not, arrange to have the American taken out of the country."

Yamir nodded. "I understand."

"Do you have money to get by?"

"Yes."

Gazli took his hand. "Farewell, my brother."

"God is great!" Yamir replied.

He watched his leader enter the elevator. The doors closed and the three Disciples of Khalfi vanished from his sight.

19

At 5:05 p.m. Bolan stepped out of the Ford on the second level of the Langton Towers parking area. He cut through the interlocking walkways and made his way down to the service-vehicle area in the basement. Emerging from the stairwell, he scanned the few parked cars, searching for the Calder Catering truck.

It was parked on the far side of the area, some distance from the access elevators that would take employees up to the hotel.

Making a wide detour, Bolan approached the vehicle from the passenger side. The truck seemed to be empty, though on closer appraisal he made out the head and shoulders of a man slumped behind the steering wheel.

Unholstering the 93-R, the warrior worked his way down the side of the truck until he was within touching distance of the driver's door. It was unlatched, slightly open, and he could hear music coming from inside the cab.

The Executioner reached out with his left hand, curling his fingers around the edge of the door panel, then yanked the door wide open.

The man sitting behind the wheel twisted around, eyes wide with alarm. He stared at Bolan for a long moment, surprise etched across his features.

"Where are the others?" Bolan demanded.

"Where you cannot stop them now," the terrorist replied. Without another word Yamir bent forward and groped under the driver's seat.

The muzzle of the Beretta angled up. Bolan stroked the trigger and delivered a cancellation note for the terrorist's visa. The impact of the round threw him across the seat. He lay there unmoving, except for one foot that twitched gently for a moment before stilling its movement forever.

Bolan took the truck keys, closed the driver's door and locked it. Checking out the cargo area, he saw that it was empty. Whatever the truck had been carrying was most probably upstairs by now.

The warrior headed for the elevator. Once inside, he punched the button for the Skylight Lounge. The descending car seemed to take forever, and inside his head Bolan could hear the relentlessly falling numbers.

The doors slid open, and the Executioner stepped out into a long corridor. At the far end double doors opened into the lounge area. He could see that the room was already crowded with guests, and he approached cautiously, eyes scanning the swell of people passing back and forth. Behind him elevator doors swished open as other guests arrived from the hotel lobby twenty floors below.

Just before the warrior reached the double doors, he saw a single door set in the corridor that was marked Staff Only. Bolan pushed against the door and felt it give. He slipped through, the door closing automatically behind him.

A short passage stretched ahead of him. At the far end, a door provided the service staff with access to the lounge. To his left was a closed door marked Changing Room Only.

Bolan put his foot to the second door and drove it wide open. He recognized the lone man in the room as one of those who had joined Rachim Gazli in the car leaving the ski lodge in Colorado.

The guy was stripped to the waist and in the process of strapping himself into the harness fitted with explosives and detonator.

As the Executioner burst in on him, the terrorist spun, shock and surprise showing in his eyes. He recovered swiftly, snatching up the Beretta 84 resting on the table beside him.

Bolan didn't hesitate. He triggered the 93-R, drilling a triburst into the human bomb's skull. The 9 mm slugs cored in deep, shattering the bone. The terrorist was flung back against the wall, his arms flying wide. He hung there a moment, then gravity drew him to the floor.

Bending over the body, the warrior removed the detonator from the device. He unclipped the fastener and dragged the harness from the body.

A door at the other end of the changing room opened without warning and a man's face appeared, his lips beginning to form a word. When he recognized Bolan, the original word was replaced by a wild yell of alarm.

Then he turned and vanished from sight, but not before Bolan was able to make out the bulky shapes under his shirt.

The guy was already wearing his device.

The Executioner straightened and sprinted after the guy.

His man was on course for the door that would take him through to the lounge and the assembled guests, but in his haste the terrorist slipped on the polished floor.

Before he regained his balance, Bolan was on him. He struck the guy sideways, the impetus of his forward motion taking the pair across the floor. They came to a stop when they hit the wall, and the warrior felt the Beretta slip from his fingers as he struggled to gain control of the situation. His main concern was stopping the terrorist from detonating the device he was wearing.

The terrorist, Abrim, fought back with silent rage. He refused to give in to this American. He wouldn't be denied his chance of greatness, his privilege of dying for his cause and eliminating the ones responsible for Ayatollah Khalfi's death.

Bolan knocked both of Abrim's arms away from his body as the man fumbled for the length of cord he needed to pull in order to complete the circuit. The warrior followed through by chopping the inner edges of his palms down against the sides of his adversary's neck. Pain flared, numbing the terrorist's shoulders. Clamping both hands at the back of Abrim's head, Bolan yanked him forward and down, slamming his upthrust knee into the man's face. Bone shattered and flesh collapsed. Abrim was flung aside, his crushed face a bloody mask of pain. He stumbled to his knees, spilling blood across the floor as he tried to drag himself back to reality, away from the agony of his damaged face. He felt hands take hold of his coat. In desperation Abrim hit out, catching Bolan in the stomach. The hands let go, and Abrim staggered to his feet, swaying dazedly. Raising his hands, he tried to wipe the blood from his eyes.

Drawing in a deep breath to counter the pain in his stomach, Bolan went after the terrorist again.

He caught his adversary as the man shook his head, the body slam spinning Abrim across the floor. Keeping in step, Bolan looped an arm around Abrim's neck, turned in toward him and swung the terrorist across his hip. Abrim crashed to the floor on his back, the breath gusting from his lungs. He struggled to rise, unaware of Bolan coming up behind him. The Executioner locked both arms around Abrim's neck and increased the pressure until the man blacked out. A moment later Bolan disarmed the bomb and bent to scoop up his Beretta.

The lounge door burst open and Rachim Gazli, attracted by the commotion, stood framed in the opening. His features twisted in bewilderment as he recognized Bolan.

"Abrim! Salim!" he screamed, his control slipping.

His right hand appeared from beneath his coat, brandishing a compact autopistol. He snapped off a quick shot that caught Bolan in the side, then turned and lunged back into the Skylight Lounge.

Pressing his hand to his bleeding side, the Executioner followed him.

Startled screams erupted from the lounge as Bolan crashed through the door.

Gazli scattered guests right and left as he crossed the floor. The autopistol cracked once, twice, sending two people to the carpet.

The Beretta in Bolan's hand swung up, the muzzle lining up on Gazli's moving figure. Ready to fire, the warrior held back as a panicked women crossed his sights.

With his line of fire suddenly clear, Bolan stroked the 93-R's trigger. A 3-round burst ripped into Gazli's left upper shoulder, reducing flesh to a pulpy mess, his thoughts of vengeance lost in the face of agonizing pain.

"Out of the way!" Bolan yelled, his commanding voice clearing a path.

Gazli had reached the double doors, stumbling against the frame as he almost went down. He broke for the corridor, recalling the fire door just yards away.

He had the presence of mind to turn and trigger a couple of shots back toward the lounge, driving his enemy to cover for a few precious seconds.

As the terrorist threw himself at the fire door, the elevator doors at the far end of the corridor slid open, and a group of people stepped out.

From the silence of the elevator, they were confronted by the chaos that reigned within the lounge.

The man at the head of the group, Jerry Brookner, turned to glance at Jack Grimaldi.

"What the hell is this?" he asked.

Grimaldi, pulling his own handgun, shouldered the journalist aside as he saw Mack Bolan striding along the corridor.

"Striker?"

Bolan glanced his way, one hand planted against the fire door.

"Keep them up here, Jack," he said. "And get Brognola."

"Hey, I need to know what's going on," Brookner demanded.

Bolan locked eyes with him. It was for only a fraction of a second, but enough to silence the man.

And then the Executioner was gone, through the fire door.

"What's going on?" Brookner asked again, this time in a quieter tone.

"It's your lucky day," Grimaldi replied.

"What?"

"For once in your life, mister, be glad you were late to your own damn party. Any earlier, and you might have been killed."

GLISTENING DROPS OF BLOOD stained the concrete steps of the stairwell. Bolan paused more than once to listen, hoping to pick up the sound of Gazli's footsteps, but there was no sound from below.

The warrior had descended three floors before he picked up the merest whisper of sound.

The bloodstains were growing in size. Gazli was bleeding badly now. The blood loss was bound to have an effect on his ability to stay ahead of his pursuer.

Leaning against the steel railing, Bolan scanned the next flight of steps. He could see more blood there, so his quarry had got that far at least.

On the next landing Bolan stopped a moment to wipe the sweat from his face. He jammed his hand over his bullet wound, feeling blood seeping from it. The scrape of shoe leather against concrete reached the Executioner's ears. He leaned over the rail, picking up the sound of labored breathing. A shadow moved below him. Bolan pulled back.

A shot rang out, and the bullet struck the rail where Bolan had been resting.

He pressed on, staying away from the rail as he slid along the wall, the Beretta tracking ahead of him.

Two more floors.

Bolan heard voices overhead and cursed mentally. All he needed was some gung ho security guards throwing their hands into the game.

Far below, steel doors crashed open.

If Bolan could hear, then so could Gazli. And the man was smart enough to realize he was trapped. If anything, that was liable to make him more dangerous than ever. He would be determined not to be taken alive, and would attempt to kill as many of the "enemy" as he could before he was gunned down.

Bolan didn't want anyone else getting hurt. Too many had already suffered because of Rachim Gazli.

He moved on, faster now, ignoring the pain in his side, fighting against the nausea.

Gazli was waiting on the next landing, slumped against the wall, his face drawn and pale. Blood soaked his shirt to the waist from the exit wounds Bolan's bullets had opened.

The gun in the terrorist's hand hung muzzle down. When he became aware of the Executioner's presence, he raised his head.

"This time you have stopped us. But it will not end, American. Soon you will realize how many of us there are. You will not stop us every time."

With a yell of pure defiance, Gazli raised his gun, then stared down the dark muzzle of the Executioner's weapon.

He had time for one swift breath of prayer before the mortal world vanished in a burst of light and became the eternal darkness he had always secretly dreaded.

EPILOGUE

Cumbria, England

Heavy rain-filled clouds hung low over the sweeping hills and valleys of the Cumberland Lake District. A cool breeze soughed down the sweep of green and rattled the branches of the trees surrounding the low-lying stone house. Following the wind came a fine mist of rain. It drove against the weathered stone and peppered the glass of the windows with droplets.

The noise disturbed the man seated at the large oak desk in one corner of the living room. He raised his head and watched the rain sliding down the glass. After a moment he stood and crossed the room to stand before the wide, open hearth where logs burned brightly, throwing a pleasant heat into the room.

Watching the flames, the man sighed. It was a sound of contentment. For the first time in weeks he felt genuinely relaxed, fully at ease with himself and the world. He stretched lazily and moved to where a polished wood liquor cabinet stood against the wall. He poured himself a tumbler of twelve-year-old Scotch whisky, sniffing the smooth aroma before taking a long swallow. The mellow liquid slid down easily. He took the tumbler back with him to his desk and sat in the comfortable leather chair. The tumbler was placed to one side as he resumed his checking of the documents laid out before him.

Another few weeks and all his financial undertakings would be transferred to his Swiss bank. Once there, they would be safe from anyone interfering with them. In the meantime he had enough cash and accounts in a number of countries to live on comfortably.

Something caught his eye. He reached across the desk and pulled it to him. Staring at it he began to smile, which turned to a soft chuckle as he studied the U.S. passport he was holding.

The face staring back at him was his own.

The name was different, though. The passport gave his name as Cecil Rogers.

In reality his name was Mason Tarantino.

His removal from the U.S. had begun in the wake of the termination of the Disciples of Khalfi strike team. Word, as always, had gotten back to him that things were heating up. Tarantino had already realized the error of dealing with the terrorists. In the beginning it had been just another deal for weapons and explosives, his daily bread, nothing out of the ordinary for a man like Tarantino. But as the situation started to deteriorate, with the elimination of the Disciples by some unknown, lone hit man, Tarantino began to wish he'd stayed well away from the Islamic group.

First the major strike at the Disciples' Chicago headquarters, followed by the disastrous attempt by the Disciples to free their injured brother from the hospital. That had turned into a bloody fiasco. From there the whole thing went downhill, culminating in a shoot-out at a major hotel in Anaheim. Tarantino's information network had fed him details of the proposed cleanup following the wipeout of the Disciples—including the fact that he was on the list of wanted people.

The message had gotten to him with hours to spare. Tarantino still had friends in high places, and they owed him for past favors and for future dealing. Even so, he had barely made it. He'd had contingency plans already prepared, including fake ID, every piece of documentation known to man. Tarantino had pressed the panic button and his organization had swung into action. By a circuitous route he had exited the U.S., traveled across Canada and caught a plane for Ireland. There his contacts in the IRA had arranged for him to enter Great Britain, and a week later he was installed in the isolated house where he was now sitting out his enforced retirement from America and reestablishing his business.

In truth it made no difference where he resided. Tarantino—now Rogers—could carry on with his arms dealing from any spot on the globe as long as he had access to a telephone and a fax machine. He had both in the house. Everything the best money could buy. With his high-tech equipment and his laptop computer holding all his contact names and numbers, Mr. Rogers could keep on wheeling and dealing.

The house had been purchased for him some twelve months back. Equipped with its own generator, food supply and satellite dish, the house was self-sufficient and isolated. The nearest village was fifteen miles away. It was a different life-style than Tarantino had been used to in Santa Fe, but infinitely preferable to languishing in a jail cell.

After the first couple of weeks he had become used to the quiet and solitude of the place. The natural beauty of the landscape wasn't lost on him. Tarantino had never been attached to anywhere to the point where it hurt to leave. He had always been a wanderer, restless, a seeker of new horizons, and he was used to packing his bags and heading off to the other side of the world on business. Yet he found he could easily adjust to the Cumbrian backwater. The longer he was there, the better he liked it.

The man wasn't entirely alone.

He had three bodyguards with him. Two had accompanied him from the U.S. and one he had picked up on arrival in Great Britain. They might not have shared his love of the place, but they were prepared to put up with it for the kind of salary Tarantino paid.

He still maintained information links with a number of agencies in the States. His contacts kept him informed of developments, and Tarantino realized that he was still being sought by the authorities.

But they had been unable to locate him.

Tarantino didn't fool himself into believing they would quit. The U.S. government had a long arm and its minions would keep looking. But he was safe enough where he was for the time being, and he had emergency plans ready if he needed to quit this place in a hurry.

In the meantime he would carry on, buying and selling, doing what he was best at.

And the hell with everyone else.

THE SUDDEN RAIN MISTED the green slopes, obscuring visibility and making it hard to see very far.

Bernie Vetch huddled into the waterproof jacket and pulled the hood farther down his face. He didn't give a damn for this piece of real estate. He clamped his big hands around the squat shape of the Ingram MAC-10 and tramped miserably across the grass, his eyes seeking out the shape of Stan Meecham, the Briton Tarantino had employed as a third hardman. Meecham, ex-British Marine, though a native of the island, hated the weather with an intensity bordering on paranoia. When it rained he turned sour, constantly grumbling and berating the country and its lousy climate. In the end, like Vetch and Spader, the third man, Meecham accepted the discomfort when he was reminded about the money being deposited in his chosen bank account.

By the time he reached the walled-off boundary of the grounds, Vetch was starting to become concerned. His bitching apart, Meecham was a solid, dependable sentry. He always maintained his patrols, keeping his time to the second. Now he was over three minutes late. The fact unsettled Vetch.

He pulled out the compact transceiver and keyed the transmit button.

"Yeah?" Spader asked. He was on the inside this shift. "Something?"

"Maybe," Vetch answered. "Haven't made contact with Meecham. He's running to four minutes over. That isn't like him. He's never late."

"Take a look around, Vetch, but keep me informed. I'll secure the house."

Vetch returned the transceiver to his pocket. He cocked the Ingram and headed off along the route that Meecham walked. If everything was okay, he should make contact with the man sooner or later.

That contact came sooner. A minute later Vetch came across Meecham's body facedown in the grass. His jacket glistened with rain, and the back of his skull, exposed and burst apart, glistened with blood.

A swell of fear clutched at Vetch's insides. he felt his stomach turn, and he fumbled the Ingram into position, turning to peer around him. He cursed the fine rainfall, which turned everything hazy, blotting out whole sections of the landscape behind a misty curtain. Vetch suddenly realized he was completely exposed, with no substantial cover for any distance.

The only consolation came from the fact that because of the falling rain, whoever was out there wouldn't be able to see any better than he could.

Right?

Yeah, right.

In the split second before he died Vetch imagined he saw a wink of light, some distance away. On the lower slope of the closest hill.

Only for an instant.

And then something struck him directly between the eyes and the world shut down forever.

"MR. TARANTINO, I think we might have a problem."

Tarantino took the statement seriously. He knew Spader very well, and Spader was rock solid, never given to panic attacks or overstating the obvious.

Pushing his chair back, he stood and went through to the side room where Spader ran his security setup.

"What is it?"

"Looks like we might have visitors. Vetch called a couple of minutes back. Said Meecham was late. I tried calling Meecham. Nothing. And now Vetch has gone off air."

"Damn!" Tarantino thought for a moment. "Teaches you not to get too comfortable. Okay, Spader. Go take a look around. I'll keep in contact."

"Yes, sir, Mr. Tarantino."

Spader pulled on a waterproof jacket and a Yankees baseball cap, then slipped a transceiver into a pocket. He picked up the AK-74 he kept beside him at all times and headed for the door.

Mason Tarantino stayed well away from any of the windows. He kept the door in view, placing himself with his back to one of the thick stone walls.

He could have allowed anger to cloud his judgment, to overwhelm him. Instead he stayed in control, using the time to plan ahead. He wasn't dead yet, and as long as he *did* have life in him he would keep on fighting. It didn't matter who was out there. Or how many. If they wanted him, they were going to have to be damn fast.

The transceiver in his hand crackled. Spader's voice came through with the hiss of the rain in the background.

"I found them, Mr. Tarantino. They're both dead. Head shots. I'd say someone took them out from a distance."

"You see anything out there?"

"No, sir. I'm on my way ba—"

The transmission ceased abruptly. Tarantino was sure that just before the contact went he heard a soft bang.

He also knew that Spader wouldn't be coming back.

Tarantino threw the transceiver across the room, then returned to his desk in the other room. It appeared he was going to have to initiate his emergency plan sooner than later, after all.

An attaché case packed solid with cash lay in a drawer of the desk. He took it out and placed it on the floor, then pulled a suitcase from the hall closet, already packed with clothing, shoes and all the identity papers he'd need, plus a passport in yet another name.

Tarantino switched off his laptop computer and zipped it away in its leather case. He stared around the comfortable room, and for a fraction of a second regretted having to leave it. But he didn't hesitate for long. He could always find somewhere else to live. Once he was dead nothing would matter.

He was about to pick up the attaché case when he sensed he was no longer alone. The arms dealer felt a cold draft of air and realized that the front door was open. Wind and rain drifted into the house, taking the edge off the warmth of the living room.

Tarantino scanned the room. He saw nothing but knew he wasn't the only one in the room.

Then he saw the tall, black-clad figure standing on the far side of the fireplace, cloaked by the soft light there.

The man's dark hair glistened with rain. He turned slowly, his face etched with hard shadow lines, the blue eyes colder than any rainstorm. His right hand appeared, holding a large automatic pistol that was aimed at Tarantino.

"Who the hell are you? And why are you here?"

"You know the answer to both those questions, Tarantino."

The muzzle of the .44 Desert Eagle lifted a fraction. "I'm your executioner, Tarantino. And I'm here because your conscience needs clearing."

The arms dealer knew he wouldn't make it, but tried anyway, scrambling for the Browning Hi-Power in the top drawer of the desk.

Bolan's big pistol thundered, filling the room with its awesome sound. The burst of fire tore off the top of Tarantino's skull, dumping the arms dealer in a bloody heap on the floor.

"It's clear now," Mack Bolan said softly, then turned and walked out of the house, back into the rainstorm.

Exiles from the future in the aftermath of the apocalypse

JAMES AXLER

DEATH LANDS®

Bloodlines

In BLOODLINES, Ryan Cawdor, off on a trek with his son, fends off the dangers from marauders and nature's traps, but also finds signs of hope for humanity's new future. Until the ultimate threat comes upon them in an unguarded moment, shocking in its scope....

In the Deathlands, nothing is as it appears.